WHAT THE EARL OF BOURNE WANTED WAS THE PLEASURES OF PEACE.

What he got, however, was a young lady who seemed bound and determined to reduce his ideally ordered existence to a state of perfect bedlam.

WHAT MISS JANE MAITLAND WANTED WAS HER FREEDOM.

What she got, however, was a marriage contract that made her the virtual property of a man who firmly believed that only she was bound by marriage vows.

Clearly Lord Bourne had to find a way to tame his outrageously unconventional bride. Clearly Jane had to find a way to turn the tables on her confoundedly conventional husband. And most clearly of all, the one thing neither should do was surrender to the enemy that would defeat all their splendid stratagems—the internal traitor known as love. . . .

THE BELEAGUERED LORD BOURNE

SIGNET Regency Romances You'll Enjoy

THE
BELEAGUERED
LORD BOURNE

MICHELLE KASEY

A SIGNET BOOK

NEW AMERICAN LIBRARY

Prologue

Snap!

The loud, discordant sound sent a flock of nesting birds, who had just moments before been chirping merrily in the branches overhead, soaring into the sky as one, calling anxiously to each other as they flapped their wings in agitation.

The girl, on the contrary, made no move to flee from the unmistakable sound of an animal trap's heavy metal jaws snapping shut, locking its unwary prey in a grip of iron. It wasn't that she hadn't felt the impulse to flee. Indeed, her heart was pounding nineteen to the dozen with fright and her muscles were quite painfully tense, silently screaming the message "Run!"

But while her spirit and flesh were willing, they could not travel anywhere as long as one decidedly heavy, extremely cumbersome animal trap had its jagged-toothed mouth stuffed full of last year's yellow sprigged muslin.

The power of speech, momentarily lost, returned just in time to give vent to the overwhelming anger that set the trapped female to trembling as the violence of that emotion rocketed through her system. "A trap in the Home Wood!" she announced incredulously to the air, pointing out the obvious to the world at large. "Never—*never*—has there been trap nor snare in the Home Wood.

Only a monster would choose to do murder to a two-pound rabbit with a five-pound trap. It's like ... it's like ... like hunting down field mice with field *cannon*, that's what it is."

Bending from the waist, she attempted to free her skirts from the offending device, but to no avail. The skirt of her gown now rent in several places (long, jagged tears that would bring tears to the eyes of the most clever needlewoman), she had no recourse left to her but to drop to her knees and scrabble about in the damp undergrowth for the stake that held the trap in place.

It took a dozen mighty tugs and a good deal of digging in the soft black soil with her bare fingers to separate the metal stake at the end of the chain from its snug home a full foot deep in the ground; a hot, sweaty business that stained her gown, dirtied her cheeks, and succeeded in enraging her to the point that the thought of her rather bizarre appearance did not deter her for so much as an instant as she set off hotfoot for Bourne Manor, dragging the heavy trap, chain, and iron post along behind her willy-nilly.

Chapter One

The large, multipaned glass doors in the morning room provided a pleasant view of the rear prospect of Bourne Manor, and Lord Bourne, wineglass in hand, debated the merits of having his luncheon served on the flagstone terrace accessible through these same doors.

After only five days in his new home, Christopher Wilde, known to his intimates as Kit and now the Eighth Earl of Bourne, felt completely at ease in his new surroundings. Renfrew, the late earl's longtime majordomo, had already proved himself to be a pearl beyond price by anticipating his new master's every need, deftly guiding his lordship until he became familiar with the layout of the large manor, and presenting him with a deceptively offhand yet amazingly thorough accounting of just what responsibilities went hand in glove with his new title.

The household servants, their company numbering in Kit's estimation just slightly less than that of Wellington's largest division, all seemed to know just what they were about. The manor being a model of organization, they took pride in considering the care and comfort of their master to have priority over polishing, straightening, and the like. Unpleasant memories of broom-wielding housemaids invading his chamber while he was still abed and important papers misplaced by overzealous servants in pursuit of domestic order reinforced his high opinion of his late uncle's staff.

Leon, Kit's valet of six years' standing, had seconded his master's vote of approval, stating unequivocally that, save for the shabby state of the Home Wood—a problem already discussed, and with corrective steps having been initiated immediately as per his lordship's directive designating his trusted valet to be in full charge of the project—Bourne Manor was "as near to perfect as a body could expect to get without first croaking and sprouting wings like."

The peaceful scene spread before him now, with rich, golden sunlight lending an added brightness to the gently rolling carpet of soft greenery and the seemingly randomly placed neat groupings of several varieties of flowers, ornamental shrubs, and small trees, made it somewhat less than difficult for Kit to convince himself that he had indeed somehow stumbled into paradise.

Reluctantly Lord Bourne restrained the urge to congratulate himself yet again for having had the good fortune to recover from the wounds he sustained in battle, thereby living to enjoy this truly magnificent day (not to mention having displaced the memory of his very ordinary leave-taking of Dame England as a mere major by means of his returning to her bosom a full-fledged earl), and was about to summon Renfrew when a movement in the extreme distance caught his eye.

Stepping closer to the window, he leaned his head forward and peered intently at the vague yellow blot that was even then advancing up the slight incline with all the grace of a knock-kneed pachyderm afflicted with a bad case of annoying heat rash.

As the blot slowly gained ground, the masses of yellow separated themselves into a large expanse of some patterned material that obviously was a woman's morning gown (and sadly lacking in style, if he was any judge), and a smaller mass of wavy golden hair that surrounded the female's head like some misshapen halo and reached considerably below her shoulders, the desired effect possibly an illusion of informality that fell sadly short, appearing instead as merely unkempt.

But what's this? Kit asked himself, his attention caught by the curious sideways slant of the female's skirts and the occasional glimpse of what seemed to be a jumble of dark, heavy-looking objects attached to those same skirts. Fumbling with the latch on the glass door, Kit stepped out onto the terrace and cupped his hands around his eyes as he inspected this oddity in earnest. What he saw caused him to issue a short, pithy curse, bound down the broad stone stairs two at a time, and pelt headlong down the grassy slope only to skid to a halt before the advancing female.

"How in bloody blue blazes did you get yourself caught in an animal trap, woman? That thing could have taken your leg off. Good God, have you no common sense? Don't you even know enough to watch where you're putting your feet when walking in the woods?" Clearly Lord Bourne's questions and general tone of mingled anger and disgust could lead his listener into supposing the man believed himself to be addressing a hard-of-hearing idiot who should even now be down on her knees giving thanks to the gods on high for her lucky escape.

Just as clearly, the recipient of his lordship's

recriminations believed she had somehow stepped
out of the woods only to stumble headlong into
Bedlam, where she was immediately accosted by
one of the hospital's more violently disposed resident lunatics.

"I," she countered, once recovered from the shock
of the man's uncalled-for attack, "am attached to
this heinous instrument of torture and murder
because some twisted, demented monster bent on
destroying poor defenseless rabbits and furry little squirrels and other such *wild and dangerous
beasties* has seen fit to set inhumane traps in the
Home Wood. *That's* how I became caught in this
contraption.

"As to my *leg,* as you have so crudely seen fit
to bring that appendage into this discussion, it
and its mate are cognizant of their narrow escape, which is most probably why they agreed to
carry me to Bourne Manor in order that I might
confront Lord Bourne with the consequences of
his thoughtless act."

"*I* am Lord Bourne, madam," Kit interjected at
this point, his bow a mere mockery as he relin-
quished neither his belligerent pose nor his menacing expression. "The traps were set in order to
thin the vermin population in the Home Wood. A
population that through lack of sensible contain-
ment threatens to outstrip its food supply, inflict
extensive damage upon the wood itself, and cause
the invasion of nearby cultivated fields where
those same cute, furry innocents will proceed to
steal seed and destroy growing crops. That the
perimeters of the area were not posted is an
oversight possibly explained by the fact that resi-
dents of Bourne Manor have been duly made
aware of the traps, while trespassers can only be
prepared to suffer the indignities of any unin-
vited guest."

"Why, you—" the young woman began hotly, then changed her tactics. "I have been accustomed to making free of the standing invitation issued me by the last Lord Bourne to think of the Home Wood as my own, as it were, and was therefore not aware that my formerly peaceful retreat had overnight taken on the aspect of a forest teeming with snapping iron dragons. Indeed, all that is missing are the tongues of fire."

"Your apology is duly noted and accepted," Kit returned cordially, his initial anger abating at the sight of the blond, green-eyed vixen who dared debate him as an equal while mud dried into crusts on her cheeks and her gown was held captive by an "iron dragon."

The young woman's jaw dropped in astonishment. "Apology? What apology? I issued no apology! I'm here to insist you remove your traps at once. They're inhuman!"

"They're not intended for humans," Kit was forced to point out. "But I do believe Leon showed an excess of zeal in setting such formidable traps. I shall amend my order to eliminate metal traps and replace them with more humane devices that ensnare rather than chomp. The end result is the same, of course," he reminded her with a satisfied smirk. "Rabbits in the larder and the vermin population reduced to manageable proportions. It is moderation that I strive for, after all, not total annihilation."

"And my use of the Home Wood?" She hated to beg, but had to ask. "Am I to discontinue my visits?"

Kit looked down at the dirt-streaked face, appealing even through its grime as the green eyes rounded artlessly and the firm little chin, so proudly tilted while she attacked him, trembled involuntarily as she awaited his answer.

"I cannot find it in myself to deprive infants of their treats. But curtail your visits for a few days, please—just until Leon gathers up his little toys."

With nothing else left to say, the young woman made to depart the scene, but the clinging trap made the simple art of turning about a test of balance and dexterity. The sprigged muslin, already laboring under considerable stress, proved unequal to this additional insult and yet another long tear split the fabric, this time exposing a wide, knee-high expanse of white petticoat.

Tears born of frustration combined with a belated but none the less extreme sense of embarrassment made liquid pools of the girl's eyes as Lord Bourne stooped to tug at her gown in an effort to release it from the trap.

"I'll have to rip your gown even further, I'm afraid," he apologized, raising his head to smile at her consolingly. "Not," he mumbled as the abused fabric parted in two, leaving a goodly yard or more still in the possession of the half-circle of grinning iron teeth, "that it's much of a loss anyway."

It is truly amazing how quickly a woman's tears can dry, leaving behind them a pair of eyes alight with a strange glitter more reminiscent of leaping flames than of sparkling water. "You owe me for this gown, Lord Bourne," she pronounced in a determined voice. "It was my very most favorite gown in the whole world!" she vowed passionately, her quest for retribution investing the lie with the ring of truth.

A healthy desire for his lunch combined with a sincere wish to be shed of his unpleasant trespasser prompted Lord Bourne to count out his astonishingly accurate estimate of the gown's cost into her outstretched palm.

And then the young woman smiled, a simple exercise of muscle that lifted the heretofore sullenly downturned corners of her mouth and reassembled the smudged contours of her face into a composition so wonderfully appealing to the eye that Kit had to blink twice before he could be assured the transformation was not due merely to a trick of the sun.

"What's your name, infant?" he heard himself ask in a soft voice, his gaze never leaving her face.

The smile wavered slightly, then rebounded. "Jennie, my lord," she answered saucily, tilting her head and throwing him an impudent wink. "I live at the far end of the Home Wood with my father."

"No last name, Jennie?" his lordship pursued, all thought of his lunch forgotten in light of this unexpected pleasant development. The girl, he decided, might clean up to advantage, and a liaison with a comely, conveniently local wench could only serve to enhance his already comfortable existence.

She was the only child of her widowed schoolteacher father, Jennie informed him conversationally, and thus the recipient of that father's intensive tutoring—a little fillip she offered to explain her accent-free, educated speech. She had read extensively, although she had never traveled more than fifteen miles from her birthplace, and even though she led a solitary existence she was more than content with her lot in life.

As she let her voice ramble on, her words tumbling out rapidly, she ran her spread fingers through her disheveled blond curls and smoothed her damaged gown with unconsciously provocative strokes of her figure-sculpting hands.

Kit had been without a woman for nearly a month, a lengthy period of abstinence for one of his healthy appetites, and Jennie's attractions multiplied in direct proportion to the estimated total number of pleasures denied. As a gentle buzzing in his ears turned Jennie's droning voice to the sweet notes of a siren's song, Lord Bourne's better self offered no resistance when his baser self reached out and drew the girl's slight form into his strong embrace.

"Let me taste your honey, sweetings," he whispered, his eyes already shut tight as his mouth descended to claim Jennie's shock-slackened lips. Kit Wilde was ever the sort to strive for excellence in his many pursuits, and he was justly proud of his carefully learned and studiously applied expertise in the art of making love.

It was perhaps a shame that Jennie had no way of comparing Kit's technique with that of some lesser mortal's, but as a first kiss it set a standard that only a few foolhardy souls might ever presume to better.

The surprise that temporarily immobilized Jennie enabled Kit to gain a secure hold on her person, a hold that proved invulnerable to any amount of squirming and frantic wriggling on her part once surprise turned into indignation and then, as his plundering mouth touched off a series of intense miniature explosions throughout her body, into very real fear.

Oblivious to it all stood Lord Bourne, his legs slightly apart, one knee thrust boldly between her slender thighs, his hands roving freely through tangled curls and along the long curving sweep of her spine as he employed lips, teeth, and tongue to their best advantage.

Unconsciously holding her breath all the while, Jennie was slightly giddy, her vision hazy and dim around the edges by the time Kit remembered their exposed situation—placed as they were within clear view of dozens of manor windows—and put a reluctant period to an interlude that had proved intensely pleasurable, if somewhat unsettling.

For the first time Jennie looked at Kit, *really* looked at him, and she realized that the new Lord Bourne was an extremely handsome gentleman of no more than eight and twenty years, a man whose quietly elegant dress displayed to advantage his moderately tall, sleekly muscular body.

As for his face, how she could have overlooked for even an instant those intensely blue eyes or that healthy crop of thick midnight-dark hair was beyond her comprehension. The lean, clean lines of his face were complemented by the almost too perfect chiseled square jaw that a wide, full-lipped mouth did little to soften. Taken in part, he was an impressive enough specimen; taken as a whole, the man was enough to give pause to the strongest heart.

How had she allowed her anger to blind her to the danger that exuded so visibly from every pore of Lord Bourne's body? Even worse, what nearsighted imp of insane arrogance had cozened her into believing she could dare to flirt with this obvious man of the world?

Acknowledgment of her own guilt in leading the earl to believe she was forward kept Jennie from either slapping Kit's face for his impertinence or dissolving into maidenly tears—as any well-brought-up young lady should have (any, that is, who had not yet taken refuge in a swoon).

In the short minute that had passed since the termination of their nearly one-sided embrace, neither of them spoke. They just stood there and stared at one another, each intent on their own chaotic thoughts.

Just as Kit was about to suggest renewing their acquaintance that night in some more secluded spot, visions of a cozy, candlelit supper followed by a mutually satisfying voyage of discovery upon the great barge of a bed in his private chamber, Jennie took him completely unawares by wheeling about, hiking up her tattered skirts, and racing pell-mell into the Home Wood.

"Wait!" Kit called, watching in amazement as her fleeing form was quickly enveloped by the dense growth and concealing shadows. "Jennie, you silly chit. Wait!"

No good would be served by pursuit, as the girl probably knew every tree and concealing rock and could elude him almost without effort. Besides, if he gave chase she might sacrifice prudence for speed, thus putting herself in danger of springing yet another of Leon's deadly traps.

Ah well, he decided, shrugging his wide shoulders, it wasn't as if she were about to disappear from his life forever. He had only to question the resourceful Renfrew as to the whereabouts of one blond-haired miss named Jennie and he would be halfway home. Once he located her, it shouldn't take more than a few soothing words (and perhaps a bauble or two) to coax the fair Jennie into his bed.

Secure in his estimation of both Jennie's character and the attractive lures his title and fortune must represent to someone of her modest circumstances, Kit returned to the manor, par-

took of a restorative luncheon, and then repaired
to the library, where he penned his acceptance of
one Sir Cedric Maitland's invitation to dine with
him the following evening.

Chapter Two

"Miss Jane, iffen ya don't stop squirmin' about like some pig caught in a gate I ain't never gonna get these tangles out, and Miss Bundy, that old cat, she'll have my head on a platter iffen you be late comin' down to table tonight. Just the thought of Miss Bundy tearin' inta me is more than I thinks I can bear."

As this whining complaint by her maid, Goldie, was reinforced by means of a restraining tug on one of those tangled locks of hair, a tug that brought tears of pain to her eyes, Miss Jane Maitland subsided obligingly onto her chair and allowed her hair to be twisted into a loose knot on the top of her head. "And woe be to anyone who doubts that the meek shall inherit the earth," Jane confided to her reflection in the mirror. "Forgive me, Goldie, my love," she said more loudly. "Far be it from me to be the cause of your catching the sharp edge of my dear companion's tongue."

"That's good," sighed Goldie, putting the last touches to her mistress's coiffure. "Seein' as how that woman's got a tongue would clip a hedge."

"Not to mention a pair of ears that can pick up the sound of your foolish jabbering at a hundred paces, more's the pity," pointed out Miss Ernes-

tine Bundy herself, who had entered the large
bedchamber unnoticed.

"Yoicks and away!" Jane chortled as Goldie
hastily hiked up her skirts and propelled her
ample girth toward the small door to the rear of
the chamber, hell-bent on escaping the peal that
Miss Bundy was otherwise bound to ring over
her poor head.

"Daft woman," Miss Bundy commented, sail-
ing into the room, her dignity in full sail. "Why
any of us put up with that sad excuse for a maid,
I find myself saying for what must be the thou-
sandth time, is far beyond my limited comprehension. Really, Jane, sometimes I feel bound to
point out to you that your grand gestures of
charity do have the lamentable tendency of pro-
ducing the most disappointing results."

"Now, Bundy," scolded Jane, rising from her
seat in front of the mirror to smooth down the
skirts of her robin's-egg-blue gown. "What Goldie
lacks in talent she more than makes up for in
heart." Twisting about to peer over her shoulder,
just making sure her departing self would do
credit to her arriving self, she went on idly, "Besides, the poor girl was such a sad failure in the
dairy."

"And in the kitchens, and as a housemaid, and
as a seamstress, and—"

"Enough, Bundy, else Papa's dinner guests will
find themselves welcoming me rather than the
other way round."

Ernestine Bundy, governess and now companion to Miss Maitland, had watched her charge
grow from an entrancingly lovely child into an
awkward, too thin adolescent until, over the course
of the year following her eighteenth birthday,
she had blossomed into the young woman who

now descended the wide stairway ahead of her: an astonishingly beautiful creature of high intelligence, quick wit, a ready smile, and a charming way about her that could coax the very birds down out of the trees.

If she was just a teeny bit strong-willed, this was only to be expected in a doted-on only child, and surely her generous nature and propensity for seeing only the good in people would never harm her as long as her fiercely protective father and Miss Ernestine Bundy were around to cushion her from some of the more distasteful realities of life.

Openly preening over her no little involvement in the creation of the exquisite creature now politely awaiting her at the bottom of the stairway, Miss Bundy had no way of knowing that one of those "realities" was already lurking in the shadows (or, in this case, in the drawing room of Maitlands itself), ready to pounce.

Lord Bourne had been at Maitlands only a few minutes—just long enough to be introduced to his host and dinner partner, be asked his preference as to liquid refreshment, have his antecedents inquired about, and his personal history vetted—all accomplished in the politest of ways and with a thoroughness a member of the Inquisition would envy.

Miss Abigail Latchwood, a spinster of some indeterminate years and, Kit assumed, a frequent visitor at Maitlands, was quite the nosiest person Kit had heretofore chanced to encounter, and he had encountered quite a few in his time. Obviously her presence tonight was Sir Cedric's way of assuring himself that news of his coup—being the first of his circle to host the new earl under

his roof—would reach even the farthest corners
of the neighborhood with all possible speed.

All in all, Kit found himself to be incredibly
bored with the whole affair, and took rapid inventory of his brain, searching for a plausible
excuse that would get him shed of Sir Cedric and
his inquisitive guest immediately after brandy
and cigars. The benighted countryside around
Bourne was a far cry from the frenetic activity of
a Spanish battlefield, and the soldier in Kit was
not so easily mellowed that the boring duties of
his new title could yet be borne with any real
grace.

If only the so-estimable Renfrew had been more
helpful in the matter of Jennie, the teacher's
daughter—that normally helpful man having dis-
claimed any knowledge of either father or off-
spring residing in the area. There were two Jessies
in the village, and the blacksmith had a niece
named Jackie visiting this month or more—although that damsel had hair as dark as pitch
and weighed half again as much as the smithy—
but nary hide nor hair could be found of any
blond wench named Jennie.

Ah well, thought the earl, smiling politely as
Sir Cedric described in great detail his latest
triumph on the hunting field, he'd be leaving for
London within another week and Jennie's bu-
colic beauty would soon fade from his memory, to
be replaced by one or more of the many comely
opera dancers he intended to honor with his favor.

Kit allowed a half-smile to soften his features
as he swirled his drink and thought his private
thoughts. Boring dinner partners and a nonexistent social life were a small price to pay for the
opportunity to call Bourne Manor his own. For a
certainty it beat wallowing in the mud of Ciudad

Rodrigo all to sticks—and the rank of earl brought
with its benefits no mere major could dream to
command.

While the aging Miss Latchwood preened delightedly, the proud Sir Cedric recounted his bril-
liant outmaneuvering of some hapless fox, and
Lord Bourne smugly contemplated a season of
wallowing in the fleshpots of London, Miss Jane
Maitland stood outside the drawing-room doors
enduring her companion's last-minute adjustments
to her charge's perfectly draped skirts.

"Papa will demand to know the reason for my
tardiness, Bundy," Jane warned her companion,
just now fussing over a loose thread daring to
peek below the hem of the blue gown, "and demand an explanation for it. I shall be forced—for
you know I would not be so mean as to implicate
you voluntarily—to explain that my companion
delayed my appearance by some fifteen minutes
while she searched out nonexistent flaws in my
toilette." Jane heaved her shoulders in a heavy
sigh. "And then Papa will rant and bluster, and I
will have recourse to tears, and you will be called
for and roundly scolded for your impudence in
thinking there existed even a single flaw on the
person of his only daughter, and then you will be
cast posthaste out into the snow—"

"It hasn't snowed in Bourne for three years,"
Miss Bundy was moved to point out, placing her
hands on Jane's shoulders and pushing her in a
circle as her shrewd eyes made one last appraisal.
"You are to dine with the new Earl of Bourne,
missy," she went on, heedless of Jane's sudden
harsh intake of breath, "and I am under strict
instructions that you are to look your very best
for the gentleman. Your papa is aiming rather
high, if you ask me, which *he* certainly did not,

but I must admit Lord Bourne would have to look far and wide to find a countess as fair as you, my dear." Giving one last unnecessary pat to Jane's coiffure, Miss Bundy stood back, surveyed her handiwork, and exclaimed: "There! No mere man could ask for more."

Jane wrinkled her nose in disgust. "Are you sure, Bundy? Perhaps my *price tag* is showing. Tell me, dearest Ernestine, is the marriage settlement to match my dowry, or will Papa throw in Mama's diamonds to sweeten the pot?" A slight flush lending even more lively animation to her features, Jane goaded further, "Dearest, sweetest Bundy. First you served as nanny, then governess, then companion. I had not realized your real calling was that of procuress."

Miss Bundy did not have an immediate spasm at her charge's audacity. Indeed, she did not so much as blink her pale-gray eyes. All Miss Bundy, that long-suffering servant, did was to pinch Jane's cheeks to give them color, step back out of sight of the double doors to the drawing room, signal the snickering footman to step lively and announce his mistress to the company, and retire upstairs to the small brown bottle she kept concealed beneath her knitting. Life at Maitlands had long ago taught the woman the best way of dealing with either Sir Cedric or his audacious daughter was by prudent withdrawal. Jane would apologize, as she always did whenever her tongue ran away with her—not that the poor girl hadn't cause enough for anger, being paraded about for the new earl like a prize calf—and in the end Miss Bundy would allow her sensibilities to be mollified by way of Jane's pretty pleas for forgiveness. It was a game they played, the two of them, with Jane tugging more and more at the leash of obedience every year as she grew from submissive girl to self-sufficient young woman.

Jane waited until Miss Bundy's receding back disappeared around the curve in the stairs and then, her softly rounded chin held high, she took a deep breath, sent up a quick prayer that Lord Bourne wasn't any more of a fool than he could help, and allowed herself to be announced.

The first person she saw when she entered the candle-lit chamber was Miss Latchwood. So, she thought wryly, Papa is leaving nothing to chance. If the poor earl so much as smiles in my direction that old biddy will have the entire countryside believing we have posted the banns. Nodding pleasantly to the older woman, who winked conspiratorially back at her, Jane turned her gaze in the direction of her father, just then posing at the mantelpiece under an obscure (for good reason) artist's rendering of one of Sir Cedric's epic exploits with the Mowbray men. "Good evening to you, Papa," she intoned sweetly, dropping the man a curtsy. "Please forgive my tardiness, but the time just seemed to run away with me."

Sir Cedric, seeing before him the reincarnation of his beloved deceased wife allowed himself to be charmed into forgiving Jane for keeping him from his dinner. Taking one of her small hands into one of his own huge paws, he turned her slightly so that he could introduce her to their guest of honor.

"Lord Bourne," the proud father began, "allow me to introduce my daughter—"

"*You!*" loudly exclaimed the earl, fairly goggling at the girl as the very air between them suddenly began to crackle.

"So much for prayers," Jane muttered disgustedly under her breath as she glared at the fashionably dressed young man with the gaping jaw.

Abigail Latchwood leaned forward in her chair, her powers of intuition telling her she had chanced to secure herself a front-row seat at what should prove to be a most interesting spectacle.

"I would be more than happy to listen to your suggestions as to a solution to our problem, my lord, but I do not wish a dismal retelling of the problem itself. Do I make myself clear?"

"*You* do not wish! *I* do not wish, damn it, and since it is my feelings that concern me and I am forced to dismiss them I see no gentlemanly need to trifle over *your* paltry sensibilities."

Jane paused to mull Kit's words over a moment or two, and decided that she may have been looking at him in the wrong light entirely. Perhaps he was not the enemy. Perhaps she had been in the process of berating the only ally she had in the entire world—what with her father, Bundy, and even Goldie firmly listed among her adversaries in this matter.

"You are against this marriage plan of Papa's?" Jane asked the man now standing across from her in the herb garden, his ebony hair gleaming in the bright morning sunlight. He nodded his head in the affirmative. "Then why," she asked with a sudden return of heat, "didn't you stop Papa when he first proposed the idea last night? You don't strike me as a man who is usually at a loss for words."

Kit shook his head in astonished disbelief. "Please don't tell me you're that much of a clothhead. After your ridiculous hysterical outburst last night when we were introduced there was deuced little *I* could do to rescue the situation."

"My *outburst?*" Jane sniffed indelicately, correcting him. "I merely muttered a small involuntary verbalization prompted, my lord, by your inelegant *bellow!*"

Kit had the decency to admit to a slight lapse of his own, caused, undoubtedly, by his surprise at seeing his wild-haired Jennie parading about as the so-proper Miss Maitland. "But," he rallied quickly, "it was not I who then fell apart like soggy tissue paper in the rain and confessed to every tiny detail of our meeting at Bourne Manor—right down to that truly sickening, simpering recital of what in fact had amounted to nothing more than a simple stolen kiss. Miss Latchwood nearly swooned dead away."

"No she didn't. She wouldn't do anything so self-defeating—it might cause her to miss some juicy bit of gossip. Lord!" Jane shuddered at the memory. "I was hardpressed not to offer her the loan of my handkerchief, she was drooling so copiously."

"So you instead offered her the notion that poor, innocent Miss Jane Maitland might just have been compromised by that nasty Lord Bourne," Kit sneered. "*Lord!*" he pressed, aping Jane's exclamation. "You may as well have gone traipsing over the countryside ringing a bell, calling: 'Kit Wilde kissed me in the Home Wood; Kit Wilde kissed me in—' "

"Don't!" Jane begged, clapping her hands over her ears. "Papa never told me the names of our guests, you see, and I didn't ask, as our dinner guests tend to be limited to Miss Latchwood, Squire Handley and his sister, or the vicar, and knowing beforehand just whom I shall be facing across the table does nothing to enliven my appetite. I only found out you were to be present a moment before I was announced. Under the circumstances I believe I did my best—"

Kit plucked a stray thread off his sleeve as he interrupted wearily, "Your best? How very sad. Please, *Miss* Maitland, I beg you to refrain from bringing my attention to your shortcomings, as I am depressed enough as it is without—"

"When I am saying something, *Lord* Bourne," Jane cut in with some heat, "you will oblige me by restraining your lamentable tendency to interrupt!"

With his head still lowered, Kit raised his eyebrows and peered at his adversary. "Welcome back, my little tiger cat. I was wondering how long it would take for Jennie to loose her claws on me." Temper definitely became the chit, Kit mused to himself, admiring the flush on Jennie's cheeks and the way the slight breeze set the blond curls around her face to dancing as her agitated movements caused her casual topknot to come half undone.

Jane looked back at him in disgust. She had requested this meeting with him this morning in the hope that together they would be able to find a way out of the muddle they had bumbled into the night before, but it was obvious now that she might just as well have saved herself the bother of eluding Bundy and engaging in what that very proper lady would only construe as yet another "tryst."

"If you are quite done salving your wounded ego at my expense, I suggest we either put our heads together to find a way out of this ridiculous coil or else terminate our meeting so that you can return to Bourne Manor and barricade the doors against Papa's wrath."

If Sir Cedric's wrath were all that was to be

faced, Kit would have been more than capable of
dealing with it in short order. But no. Once Jennie (he refused to call her Jane) had been escorted to her room by the so properly outraged
Miss Bundy and Miss Latchwood had been se-
questered in the morning room with a half-
decanter of her favorite cherry brandy, Sir Cedric
had confessed to Lord Bourne that he suffered
from a "disky heart," and any scandal surround-
ing his dear only child would as surely put him
underground as would a bullet through the brain.

Kit was prompted to wonder aloud about how
such a hearty-looking specimen—a man who rode
to hounds with such vigor—could possibly be in
ill health, a tactical error that sent Sir Cedric
tottering posthaste to a nearby chair, a hand clutching at his ample bosom as he called weakly for
his manservant. While Kit looked on, his face
still showing his skepticism, Sir Cedric's solici-
tous valet administered a draught to the panting
gentleman and, with the help of two sturdy footmen, had his employer hoisted aloft in his chair
and carted off to his bed—a move that put quite
an effective period to any hope of rational discussion.

Galloping home, sans one promised dinner, the
earl had barked out orders for food and drink to
an astonished Renfrew only to react in a most
violent manner when the platter of succulent
rabbit smothered in spring onions was placed
before him, rudely tossing the rabbit, platter and
all, smack against the nearest wall. Hours later,
just before the quantity of port he had ingested
lulled the young earl into heavy slumber, Renfrew
heard his master proclaim sorrowfully: "Rabbits
are the root of all that is evil in this world. If I
were king there would not be one of the fuzzy-

tailed monsters left on this whole bloody isle. Damned if there would."

Upon awakening the next morning Kit did not remember this particular profound statement, a punishing hangover being his only lingering souvenir of a truly forgettable evening; but Jennie's note served to bring his dilemma into sharp focus and he had rallied sufficiently to agree to the meeting now taking place in the Maitland herb garden. Not that their discussion had so far produced anything more tangible than a mutual agreement as to the total unsuitability of both parties for the roles of husband and wife.

And yet, his head still pounding as if a blacksmith had set up shop between his ears, and his ears ringing with Jennie's condemning accusations, Kit found himself coming to the reluctant conclusion that his carefree bachelor days could be numbered on the fingers of one hand. There was no retreat for a man of honor, no possible avenue of escape without bidding his good name a permanent adieu. Between them, the naively candid Jennie and her determined Papa had trussed him up all right and tight and delivered him neatly into the parson's mousetrap. All that remained now was to convince his "intended" of the futility of resisting the inevitable.

"Well?" Jennie demanded, breaking into Kit's thoughts. "Have you been struck dumb?"

"While I will admit to feeling slightly less than my usual intelligent self," Kit replied, a note of bitter self-mockery in his tone, "I am not about to oblige you by descending into imbecility, as even being forced to wed you, my dear Jennie, cannot make me forget I am a Wilde, and as such above any such cowardly dodge. Not that the idea is entirely without appeal, you understand."

"Then you are going to simply knuckle under, marry a woman you obviously detest—making the both of us totally miserable in the process—rather than make the least push at settling the matter another way?" Jennie's huge eyes were staring at him incredulously.

"What other way would you suggest?" Kit asked politely, taking Jennie's hand and placing it on his arm before guiding her in a leisurely stroll along the garden path.

Jennie's brow creased in concentration as she cudgeled her brain in a quest for some splendid burst of inspiration. Sadly, none was forthcoming, and, upon reaching the gate at the bottom of the path, she admitted she hadn't a clue as to where to search for salvation.

"I'd be inclined to suggest prayer," Lord Bourne said, tongue in cheek, "but I doubt the Lord grants entreaties that have to do with transporting earls to the far side of the moon." Turning so that they faced each other fully before he uttered the fateful words, Kit then intoned solemnly, "Miss Maitland, I have admired you from the moment of our first meeting and can only hope that you have come to return my esteem at least in part. Please, Miss Maitland, do me the honor of making me the happiest man on earth by consenting to become my bride."

As a proposal of marriage it lacked nothing in composition, although condemned men must have sounded more cheerfully animated speaking their final words before mounting the scaffold. And if his mention of their first meeting was taken at face value, devoid of any intentional double meaning, Jennie supposed it was a much nicer proposal than she could have expected under the circumstances. It was not, however, the proposal she had dreamed of ever since reading her first Minerva Press romance.

If her heart beat faster, it was with the frantic flutterings of a trapped animal, and not the accelerated rhythm all romantic heroines experienced at the very sight of their beloved. If her breathing was swift and shallow, it was panic, not passion, that set her young breast to heaving rapidly up and down. And if her milky English complexion was very prettily set off by a sudden blush of dusky rose suffusing her cheeks, it should be remembered that agitation should not automatically be construed as excitement.

Jennie looked searchingly into Kit's blue eyes, searching in vain for some carefully concealed humorous glint that would assure her he had spoken in jest. She found none. He was serious, she concluded at last, deadly serious. Earls may not steal kisses from baronets' daughters, even if they thought they were merely indulging in a bit of a lark with some little nobody of no consequence. Violators, this unwritten law decreed, will forfeit either their honor or their freedom.

Lord Bourne had made his choice. He would marry her to satisfy the conventions. And to save her good name, she reminded herself nastily, she shouldn't forget that little favor—not that Bundy would ever let her.

"Well," she said at last, just when Kit was beginning to think she would turn him down flat and wildly wondering just why this particular notion should distress him as much as it did, "you aren't fat. There's that at least."

Kit smiled broadly, clasping her hands in his as something tightly coiled deep inside his chest obligingly relaxed. "I'm not bald either," he pointed out cheerfully, amused by her youthful bluntness.

Jennie returned his smile, shyly at first, and then expanding the smile into a wide grin. "Or ancient, full of prickles and complaints, and suffering with the gout."

"Or foul-smelling, or afflicted with warts, or widowed with six bawling brats for you to mother, or hard of hearing, or missing half my teeth."

"Or a dedicated gamester?"

"Not even on nodding acquaintance with the cent-per-centers, playing for sport but never too deep."

"Or overfond of spirits?"

"Moderation—moderation in all things—that's my motto!" he averred, conveniently dismissing his truly dedicated drinking of the night just past.

"Well then, a girl would be foolish beyond permission to turn her back on such an obvious catch as you, my lord, wouldn't she?" Jennie declared, her smile faltering a bit before shining as before.

At last she could see the humor lurking in Lord Bourne's twinkling eyes. "Foolish indeed, Miss Maitland," he assured her, lightly squeezing her hands.

"Then . . . then I accept your kind proposal, sir, and I thank you." The fateful words spoken, Jennie allowed her smile to fade and dipped her head, no longer able to meet Kit's all-seeing gaze.

As she stood there, doing her utmost not to tremble and thus betray her nervousness, Kit slipped his crooked index finger beneath her chin and lifted her face toward his descending head. "A betrothal must be sealed with a kiss," he whispered solemnly before laying claim to Jennie's lips with the velvet warmth of his mouth.

Remembering their first kiss—the way he had

captured her in his embrace and exercised his
considerable aptitude in the fine art of seduction—
Kit deliberately kept this kiss gentle, undemand-
ing; a tentative exploration rather than an attempt
at conquest, and Jennie responded by allowing
her lips to soften, molding themselves to fit against
his in a highly pleasing manner.

He did not wish to wed Jennie. He did not wish
to be married at all until at least a half-dozen
more years of bachelor-oriented indulgence and
high living were behind him. He resented being
pushed into matrimony at, figuratively at least,
the point of a gun, and to a mere child just out of
the nursery, no less.

Jennie Maitland was the exact opposite of the
sort of female he had hoped to surround himself
with in London. She was much too young, for one
thing, besides being woefully inexperienced—
possessing none of the brittle sophistication required to survive in the *haut ton*—and to top it
all, he decided glumly, the outside world would
consider him responsible for her well-being and
behavior.

Kit had just completed two grueling years of
volunteer duty in Spain, and he was sick to death
of responsibility—responsibility for the men who
fought and died under him, and responsibility for
the constant daily decisions of command. His
wound and his lengthy convalescence had sorely
tried his patience, with only the prospect of the
gaiety promised in the coming London Season
serving to keep a rein on his impatience until he
was free to join his friends in an orgy of hell-
raking and carousing that would set the metrop-
olis on its heels.

A wife could only be viewed as a serious im-
pediment to his plans. Husbands lacked the free-

dom of bachelors, especially brand-new, supposedly honeymooning husbands. He would marry the chit and leave her at Bourne Manor for the Season if he could, but his conscience overrode him on that score. Besides, he felt sure, Sir Cedric was not beneath another theatrical display of ill health just to force his son-in-law's hand, and Kit didn't think his constitution could bear another such performance. But going around London with a wife in train was going to be like trying to run with an anchor—or should he say "mantrap"—chained to his ankle, deuced difficult.

And yet ... and yet, he thought as Jennie allowed him to take her more fully into his arms, the child wasn't totally lacking in appeal. With proper tutoring, his tutoring, he could almost believe she'd eventually make a more than tolerable bed partner.

Suddenly Kit's appetite for romance evaporated. Of course Jennie was a kissable wench—that's how he had come to be in this damnable coil in the first place! Too much of this sort of thing and he'd not only be saddled with an unwanted wife, but he'd find himself a papa into the bargain.

Jennie looked up at him, puzzlement clouding her eyes. What was wrong? Didn't he like kissing her? She had enjoyed it quite a little bit herself, although she'd rather swallow nails than admit any such thing, but from the pained look on Kit's face he had found the entire experience distasteful. Well, she thought angrily, he had certainly taken his good sweet time making up his mind, seeing as how he had been kissing her for more than a full minute—she had counted to sixty-four, as a matter of fact, just to keep from doing something silly like throwing herself into his arms like some love-starved ninnyhammer.

"If everything is official now?" Jennie prompted, angry to hear a trace of huskiness in her voice.

"Hmm?" the earl murmured, still lost in his own depressing thoughts. "Yes, you insolent infant, everything is all right and tight," he assured her much like a parent shushing a bothersome child. "You may go inside now and wait for your luncheon and I will return at the dinner hour to speak with your father about the final arrangements—if he has recovered from his indisposition of last evening, which I am somehow convinced he has."

"Kit," Jennie called rather sharply, as Lord Bourne had already turned and begun walking toward his horse.

"What?" he questioned rudely, eager to be gone.

"You may not be fat or bald, your lordship," she trilled, spurred by a sudden need to strike back at the man who had so carelessly dismissed her, "but you neglected to mention that you possess all the charm and personality of a turnip."

Kit stood stock still as Jennie flounced off with her head held high, obviously believing herself to have come off the victor in their little sparring match, before muttering as he stomped off toward his waiting mount: "Leading strings. I'll be the only husband in London who has a wife in leading strings. Impertinent infant!"

Chapter Three

It was a wet wedding. Goldie's never-ending stream of tears, accompanied by sighs, gulps, hiccups, and several ear-shattering recourses to her oversized red handkerchief were depressing enough without nature echoing the maid's sentiments by sending dull gray skies and a drenching downpour just as the bride was leaving for the church.

Nothing is quite so inelegant as a limp lace veil unless it is a wilted, water-spotted silk gown with a muddy hem, both of which Jennie wore as she trailed reluctantly down the short aisle with Sir Cedric hauling her toward the altar with unseemly haste.

The ceremony itself was mercifully brief, with Ernestine Bundy poker-faced as the maid of honor and Leon, Kit's valet, preening pompously in his role of groomsman.

With clumps of baby rose petals clinging damply to their bodies, the bride and groom made short work of climbing into the traveling coach that stood ready to embark on the day-long trip to London, with two other smaller, less elegant coaches holding their belongings and personal servants set to follow along behind.

After handing his bride into the coach, Kit ordered his driver to head for Bourne Manor, deciding a change of clothes was necessary if their journey was to be accomplished in any degree of comfort.

Bride and groom allowed the short journey to pass in silence and parted from each other's company without regret to enter separate bedrooms and await the arrival of their servants bearing dry clothing.

A scant half hour later—the earl noting the new Lady Bourne's promptness with a pleasure he saw no need to convey to her—they were finally on their way, with Kit already bored with the confinement of the coach and wishing himself astride the spirited black stallion tied to the back of the coach and Jennie idly stroking a strange wooden carving she held lovingly in her gloved hands.

His own thoughts holding no real appeal, Kit reluctantly turned his attention to the girl perched so stiffly beside him, and his gaze alighted on the carving. "And do you plan to plummet me with that maltreated tree branch if my baser instincts surface and I attempt to ravish you here in this coach?"

Jennie gave the carving a considering look before turning her head to stare at her husband as if weighing her chances of success if she was forced to defend herself before slowly shaking her head and confessing, "I saw the carving as I passed by the main saloon and couldn't resist taking it with me as a remembrance of home."

"You consider Bourne Manor to be your home?" Kit questioned, raising his brows so that furrows formed on his smooth forehead.

Jennie shrugged her shoulders nonchalantly, replying, "The late earl encouraged me to think of Bourne Manor that way, and I was accustomed to being welcomed almost as a member of the family. He had no children, you know, and he was frightfully lonely when his wife died five years ago."

Noticing the way Jennie's tightly controlled features relaxed as she spoke of his uncle, Kit pressed on with his questions, not overly interested but conceding that a pleasant conversation was as good a time-passer as anything else he could think of at the moment. "But why that truly homely carving? You could have had your pick of the manor rather than settling for one of the scores of carvings—all looking very much like misshapen turtles with udders, by the way—that litter the place."

Jennie's shoulders straightened as she took exception to Kit's insulting remark. "I'll have you know that this carving—indeed, *all* the carvings— are very creditable renditions of Amy Belinda, your uncle's favorite model. He took great pride in his work, and I'll not sit idly by and let you malign his efforts."

"Amy Belinda?" Kit nudged.

"His pet cow," Jennie informed him matter-of-factly.

"Of course," her husband responded in a choked voice. "His pet cow." His face mirroring his astonishment, Kit prized the carving from Jennie's grasp and raised his quizzing glass to study Amy Belinda from various angles—none of which provided a clue as to which end depicted the cow's front end. "M'uncle carved this?" he puzzled. "Good God—he must have been lonely!'"

"He was not!" Jennie protested angrily. "At least he wasn't once I introduced him to Will Plum. Poor man," she mused reflectively. "Will lost his wife about the same time as the earl, and as he was too old to work as a carpenter anymore he felt he had nothing left to live for.

"Well," she went on, heedless of her husband's incredulous expression, "any fool could see the two men needed each other, and once I put Will in the earl's way the two of them became the best of good friends. Will taught the earl woodcarving and your uncle thought it was just grand to capture his dearest Amy Belinda in all of her many moods."

"Cows have moods?" Kit interrupted, not that Jennie noticed.

"Their friendship lasted for five years, until old Will finally died, your uncle surviving him by only a month. Amy Belinda didn't last much longer, poor dear," she added thoughtfully, "but I imagine that was only to be expected."

"Definitely," the earl agreed, trying hard to contain his mirth. "I had no idea I had wed such a clever puss—matching such disparate persons as my uncle and the estimable Will Plum with such gratifying results. Is this a special talent of yours, or was old Will a fluke?"

Jennie knew Kit was teasing her, but she refused to allow it to rankle. She had always prided herself on her ability to settle people into niches she personally carved out for them, deriving satisfaction by aiding her fellow human beings.

Her maid, Goldie, was a prime example of the success of her humanitarian endeavors, and so she proceeded to inform the scoffing earl. "She was totally hopeless in the dairy, you understand, being mortally afraid of cows."

"Sad," Kit commented, clucking his tongue in commiseration.

"Poor Goldie. She felt herself to be an abject failure, and her mother, a widow and dependent on Goldie for her support, came to me and begged me to take her daughter in hand."

"Naturally you agreed," Kit interjected cheerfully.

"But of course—how could anyone so petitioned do anything else?" Jennie countered emphatically. "We tried Goldie in the laundry, but the soap made her sneeze, and even I could find little to praise in her needlework. She was so dejected we could scarcely catch a glimpse of her grandest possession, for she smiled so seldom. She has a truly magnificent gold tooth smack in the front of her mouth, you know, which is why we call her Goldie even though her name is Bertha."

"This is a most affecting story. I can only wonder if I am strong enough to hear the rest," lamented the grinning earl, earning himself a killing glance from his new bride.

"I'll disregard your sarcastic attempt at humor, if only to prove my point," she told him crushingly.

"Oh? There's a point?" Kit exclaimed in disbelief. "How gratifying."

"Of course there is. The point is that there is a place for everyone if one but takes the time to seek it out. In Goldie's case the search was a bit longer than usual, as she soon proved incapable of serving at table without overturning the soup tureen or losing her grip on a stack of dirty plates. But I really had hopes for her as a kitchen assistant—you know, peeling vegetables and chopping things and such—until Papa's silly French chef threatened to hand in his notice if Goldie wasn't permanently removed from his sight."

"Got on the bad side of the fellow, I assume?" Kit opined, and Jennie vigorously nodded her agreement.

"I still don't see what all the fuss was about," she ended, her expression one of sublime innocence. "After all, it wasn't as if his mustache wouldn't grow back eventually. He removed the rest of it after Goldie's little accident with the knife, you see, which was just as well considering he looked rather lopsided with half of the droopy thing gone."

That did it. Kit was unable to contain his mirth any longer, and his full, masculine laugh reverberated inside the closed coach as he gave voice to his amusement.

Within seconds Jennie's delicious-sounding giggles blended with her husband's throaty chuckles as the two leaned against each other for support as they enjoyed the joke—causing the coachman to remark later to the postilion that Lord and Lady Bourne seemed to be taking to each other right quick-like, which was a good thing considering they was bracketed like it or nay.

After a quick stop for luncheon Jennie allowed herself to be talked into resting her head on her husband's broad shoulder, and the rest of the journey passed with Lord Bourne alternately gazing dolefully at the scenery passing by outside his window and doing his best to ignore the soft, warm bundle nestled so trustingly against his chest.

Jennie felt she had somehow been transported to another world. It wasn't as if her father's house had not been comfortable, and she had run tame at Bourne Manor for as long as she could remember, but nothing in her experience had prepared her for the opulence of the Bourne mansion—no stretch of the imagination could convince her

that this massive structure was any ordinary
townhouse.

Bourne Manor had been furnished with an eye
for comfort rather than elegance, but the many-
storied dwelling in Berkeley Square was crammed
cellars to attics with furniture and accessories
that intimidated her with their grandeur.

Even the walls and ceilings, festooned as they
were with intricate stucco designs and painted
Cipriani nymphs, seemed to mock her as she
roamed aimlessly from room to room, feeling
smaller, less significant, and increasingly more
insecure as she encountered Sheraton sideboards,
Darly ceilings, Shearer harlequin tables, Zucchi
pilasters, arches, and panels, Thomas Johnson
clocks, Chippendale parlor chairs, and even an
Inigo Jones chimneypiece that had been carted
there from heaven only knew where.

"Love a duck, miss, ain't it grand?" Goldie
gushed for the hundredth time, her eyes nearly
popping out of her head as she followed in her
mistress's wake, nearly cannoning into Jennie
before she realized the girl had stopped dead at
the entrance to the master bedchamber.

"Th-there's no need to go poking about in here,"
the new Countess of Bourne stammered nervously
before beating a hasty retreat back down the
wide hallway to her own chamber, closing the
door behind her, and leaning against it as if to
block out the rest of the world.

"Is that any way for a countess to enter a
room, racing and romping and slamming doors
behind her?" Miss Bundy, never raising her eyes
from the trunk she was in the midst of unpack-
ing, asked in her best stern-governess voice. "And
what is that infernal banging?"

Jennie opened the door an inch, saw Goldie's

hand raised for yet another assault on the heavy door, grabbed the maid's arm, and hastily pulled the plump form inside. "Land sakes, missy, what didya see in there ta set ya off like a cat in a fit?" the maid asked, darting a quick glance out the crack in the door as if to catch a glimpse of some horrifying creature barging down the hallway.

"I didn't see anything, Goldie," Jennie responded a lot more coolly than she thought possible. "I just suddenly remembered that we left poor Bundy alone all morning to unpack while we gadded about the place gawking like country bump-kins, that's all."

As Goldie had been more than aware that Miss Bundy had spent the morning toiling while she, in a very un-maid-like way, had done nothing more strenuous than inspect her mistress's new digs, and as Goldie had secretly delighted in this unaccustomed freedom, her only answer to this damning statement was to flash her gold tooth at Jennie and wink broadly before picking up a paisley shawl and making a great business out of folding it over her arm.

Thank goodness, thought Jennie, releasing her pent-up breath in a long sigh. They're both too busy either working or avoiding work to tax me further. I'll just have to learn to control myself better and not do anything else to arouse their suspicions. Why, if Goldie knew I'd been fright-ened by a mere *bed* she'd tease me to death, while Bundy would see it as ample reason for yet another blistering lecture on the punishment of "Evil"—the evil in this case having more than a little bit to do with "giving false witness" only to "reap what you have sown." Hummph! Jennie thought with a toss of her blond curls. I need

another lecture like that like I need another
freckle on the tip of my nose!

Snatching up a book from a nearby table, Jennie made her way past opened trunks and pieces
of her personal belongings Bundy had divided
into various towering piles, the purpose of which
only she knew or cared to know, and took up
residence in the deep, robin's-egg-blue velvet-
padded windowseat that overlooked the square
and the statue that depicted a much younger,
trimmer Prinny on horseback—the royal frame
all rigged out like some long-dead Roman em-
peror for reasons only Princess Amelia, who had
commissioned the piece, knew.

The book spread open on her lap (she never did
take notice of its title), Jennie let her thoughts
drift to the preceding evening and what she knew
had been the markedly less than regal London
debut of the new Countess of Bourne—considering
she had slept through the entire business.

The strain of the wedding had somehow temporarily overcome her wariness of the man she was
henceforth to love and cherish and—she gritted
her teeth as she had done when the minister bade
her repeat the word—*obey,* and against her better judgment she had allowed herself to fall asleep
against his shoulder, thereby missing her very
first sight of London by night.

It was only when the sound of hushed but
obviously angry voices intruded on her slumber
that she had roused sufficiently to realize that
she was no longer in the coach, but reclining,
cloak and all, upon an extremely comfortable
bed.

"It's indecent, that's what it is," hissed the first
voice, which Jennie had readily recognized as
Bundy's.

"God's teeth, woman, I was merely loosening the ties of her cloak, not taking the first step in any serious pursuit of debauchery," a second, masculine voice had hissed back angrily.

"Kit!" Jennie remembered she had screamed—fortunately only in her sleep-befuddled mind and not aloud. Squeezing her eyes shut, she had tried to feign sleep once more, hoping they would all just go away and leave her alone, but the earl was too sharp not to notice the sudden tenseness in the lower limb he had just then been in the process of divesting of its footgear.

"Ah ha!" he had crowed, more than a hint of triumph in his voice. "Methinks yon beauty awakes! Dash it all, foiled again. Just when I was about to have my evil way with the innocent, not to mention *unconscious*, damsel." This last was said with heavy sarcasm, which, as Jennie could have told him, sailed completely over the head of the hovering Ernestine Bundy.

That overwrought female, torn between her duty to her charge and a strong inclination to indulge herself in a bout of strong hysterics, had then somehow steeled herself to throw her body between Jennie's and that of her would-be ravisher and declared in a quavering voice, "Over my lifeless, bleeding body, *sirrah!*"

Even now Jennie's shoulders shook slightly as she remembered Kit's immediate descent into the ridiculous—clasping his hands to his chest and fervently denying any intention to harm so much as a single hair of the lady's gray head while backing toward the door mouthing absurd apologies that had Jennie stuffing her knuckles into her mouth so that she would not laugh out loud.

"I saved you for now, young lady," Bundy had told her charge as she helped her undress before throwing a nightgown in her general direction and stomping heatedly out of the room. "But I shan't always be here to protect you. Remember," was her parting shot, "you have made your bed, my dear—and now you must lie upon it!"

And lie upon it Jennie had done; long into the dark of the early-morning hours, tossing and turning but never finding her rest until a thin, watery sun rose above the horizon.

By the time Goldie had roused her with her morning chocolate, Jennie felt like the proverbial last bloom of summer—faded, more than a tad wilted, and increasingly unable to put on a brave face for yet another chilly day.

But being young, and therefore fairly resilient, by noon Jennie had been sufficiently restored in spirits for her to drag the willing Goldie on the tour that had ended abruptly at the sight of the massive bed in what she knew was the chamber she would soon be expected to occupy with her husband.

I can't do it! she shrieked silently, her small hands clenching into fists and thoroughly wrinkling the green sprigged muslin skirts now clutched between her fingers. Kit said I had to marry him. Papa said it was my duty. But I and I alone will say whether or not I have to share his bed. And I say *no!*

"Jane. *Jane!*" Miss Bundy repeated more loudly. "Woolgathering again, I suppose. Some habits never change. Why, I remember when you were seven and I found you daydreaming in that tree in the garden. I had to call you a dozen times before—"

"Before you startled me out of a very pleasant daydream, as I recall, and I toppled to the ground and broke my arm," Jennie ended for the lady. "Papa wasn't best pleased, you'll remember."

Miss Bundy merely sniffed, obviously still feeling she had been more victim than sinner in that particular incident.

"Well?" Jennie asked after some moments when Miss Bundy seemed to be lost in replaying old hurts.

"Well, what?"

"You called my name, Bundy, remember?" Jennie sighed, a small smile lighting her face as the familiarity of this little scene made her feel less an alien in an unfriendly land.

Miss Bundy puzzled a moment, tapping one long finger against her pointed chin, before declaring brightly, "I remember now. How very remiss of me. Renfrew gave me a note earlier for you—which I opened, of course—"

"Of course," Jennie sighed fatalistically.

"Don't interrupt, Jane. All my many hours of instruction on deportment and still you—but never mind. The note says that the earl desires the pleasure of your company in the main saloon—that's the huge room just off the foyer, the one that houses the Jones chimneypiece, my dear—at half past three of the clock today. My goodness, it's that now! You'd best hurry, dear, but do let Goldie straighten your hair first."

"There's no time for that, Bundy. I'm late as it is," Jennie said in reply, already moving toward the door. Now that she had made up her mind about the direction she wished this marriage to take, she was all at once bursting with the necessity to share her decision with Lord Bourne—whom she graciously acknowledged to possibly have some slight interest in the business.

The Earl of Bourne was pacing the main saloon, glass in hand, looking about him with what

he hoped was bored disinterest. This place is a
far cry from your bachelor digs in the Albany off
Piccadilly, even if Byron, Macaulay, and Glad-
stone shared the same address, Kit, my lad, he
mused, positioning himself with one arm propped
negligently (he hoped) upon the mantelpiece.

If only he could get over the disquieting feeling
that at any moment some long-lost Wilde with a
better claim to the title would come bursting
through the door and roust him outside and back
into the real world.

Kit had never dreamed he would one day inherit his uncle's title, lands, and great wealth. In
fact, the most he had hoped for—when he dared
to hope at all—was for the old boy to leave him a
broken pocket watch or some such useless trinket.

But fate works in strange ways; in this case by
eliminating all close heirs by way of accident or
unfortunate illness. And while Kit had been striving to make a name for himself as a soldier, his
male relatives had all been conveniently dropping like flies in order to pave his way to the
earldom.

And fate hadn't stopped at the earldom either.
Dame Fate, not one to indulge any mere mortal
to the point where he might tend to get cocky,
had then leavened Kit's triumph a bit by sad-
dling him with a totally unnecessary gift—a wife.

He abandoned his studied pose—his lordship
reclining at his ease—to check the watch at his
waist. His *late* wife, he pointed out to himself,
just as there came a noise at the doorway and
Jennie entered with more haste than decorum,
skidding to an ignominious halt about three feet
inside the double doors.

"I . . . um . . . I mean, *Bundy* . . . er . . . that is
. . . you wanted to see . . . um, talk to me?" Now

that's an auspicious beginning, Jennie berated herself mentally, her outward grimace bringing a pained smile to the earl's face.

Yes, infant, Kit replied silently, I do want to see you—waving goodbye as you ride out of my life. But he did not say the words. Jennie was his wife now, for good or ill, and they were just going to have to make the best of the cards Dame Fortune had so capriciously dealt them.

"Sit down, Jennie," Kit said gently, then waited impatiently as she took up her seat on a straight-backed chair positioned at the far side of the room. "Would you like me to ring Renfrew for some tea? No? Then I suggest we get right down to it."

Jennie jumped slightly—just as if he had suggested they lie down on the Aubusson carpet and proceed to make mad, passionate love—and Kit hastened to explain the reason for his summons. "We must organize this household, Jennie, as Renfrew and the skeleton staff my late uncle kept here are not sufficient to our needs if we mean to entertain during the Season."

"We mean to entertain?" Jennie asked, trying to imagine herself in the role of hostess of this great mansion and failing dismally.

"We do. Unless that presents a problem?" Bourne inquired, deliberately needling her.

"Of course it doesn't," Jennie assured him through clenched teeth, wanting nothing more than to box his lordship's ears. "I'll set about hiring extra staff as soon as possible."

"Renfrew will arrange things with a reputable agency, and you will only have to select from a group of eligible applicants." Kit saw no possible way Jennie could land in the briers with the resourceful Renfrew to guide her.

"Oh," Jennie murmured confusedly. "I had thought to place an advertisement about, as we do at home sometimes if the need arises."

Kit quickly explained the folly of ever advertizing for domestic help—heaven only knowing what sort of riffraff might then show up in Berkeley Square looking for a handout. At Jennie's nod he promptly considered the matter to have been satisfactorily settled and went on to discuss a more delicate topic—one he had been secretly dreading to broach.

"Jennie," he said gently, dropping to one knee beside her chair, "after giving the matter a good deal of thought, and with due consideration of your sensibilities and the uniqueness of our situation, I have decided not to ask for my husbandly rights just yet. I believe we should first become more comfortable with each other."

"Oh, *good!*" Jennie exclaimed happily, before she could temper her response. "That is, I mean, *why? . . . No!* Don't answer that. I don't mean *why,* exactly. Disregard that if you will, please. What I mean to say is—thank you." As Kit's eyebrows shot up, she stumbled on hastily, "No! I didn't mean that either, did I? I guess I don't mean to say anything at all, do I? I'm sorry I interrupted you, my lord," she said, belatedly striving to behave like something more than completely brainless. "Please, continue. You were saying—"

"Actually, pet, I was done *saying,*" he told her, stifling his amusement at her obvious agitation. But this amusement changed rapidly to confusion as Jennie's eyes took on a hard glint and her chin lifted in determination. "Now what?" he was then foolish enough to inquire.

Jennie, who should have been feeling nothing

less than tremendous relief, had suddenly decided that the man in front of her was nothing
less than the greatest beast in nature. How dare
he decide not to exercise his rights? How dare he
tell her anything! It was *she* who would do the
telling!

As Kit watched, Jennie's face did its little cha-
meleon trick yet again and became soft and almost pleading in its woebegone expression. "Then
you do not want me, my lord? I do not appeal to
you—perhaps even repel you?"

Looking up at her, his heart touched by her
wide, sad eyes, Kit protested passionately, "Of
course I want you, infant. You appeal to me immensely. Isn't that how we found ourselves in
this situation in the first place?"

Now Jennie smiled in earnest. Rising to look
down on her still-kneeling husband, she informed
him brightly, "That is a great pity, my lord husband. For I do not want you, which is why I was
so glad you requested this meeting. I was looking
forward to telling you that you may have taken
my hand in marriage, but that is all you will
take from me." So saying, and with her gape-
mouthed husband looking on, she swept out of
the room, at last looking every inch the countess.

Chapter Four

Kit entered the dim main room of the Guards Club and cast his eyes about in the gloom with the alert, roving gaze of a man who has served on the Peninsula. He quickly spotted and nodded to several acquaintances, but it was not until his scrutiny was rewarded with the sight of one fellow in particular that he smiled and started across the uneven sanded floor of the converted coffeehouse.

"Ozzy, you old dog," he called out loudly as he advanced on a painfully stylish young man of fashion sprawling at his ease at a table in the corner. "I knew I could count on you to be here."

Ozzy Norwood, who had just then been profoundly contemplating a fly walking backward up the table leg and wondering that such powers would be given to a mere insect and yet denied one such as himself, was so startled at this violent intrusion upon his thoughts that his legs—which had been propped on a facing chair—slid from under him and his rump took up a closer association with the hard floor.

His mood, as he had over the years become accustomed to his own clumsiness, was not darkened by his ignominious position, and he swiftly if not gracefully regained his feet in time to be caught up in Kit's enthusiastic bear hug of a greeting.

"Kit! Kit by damn Wilde! I'd heard you cashed it in at Badajoz," Ozzy exclaimed when he could get his breath. "You're no ghost, though. My bruised ribs can attest to that, by God! Let me loose, you great hairy beast, and let me look at you. What a sight you are, man."

What Ozzy saw was his old friend and fellow officer: a little leaner, perhaps; a little tougher, most definitely; but those smiling eyes were still those of the Kit Wilde Ozzy had hero-worshiped since they were both in short coats. "You look wonderful, friend, and I mean it truly. Sit down. Where did you spring from? Last I heard you were wounded and not expected to make it. I took a ball in the shoulder in a damn silly skirmish in some benighted Spanish slum village soon after Badajoz and sold out—my heart just wasn't in it, what with you gone and all—but I couldn't get word of you anywhere. It was as if you fell off the face of the earth. Girl! Bring us a bottle of your finest! Sit *down*, I said, Kit, and stop standing there grinning like a bear. Have you nothing at all to say for yourself?"

Kit could only laugh and shake his head. "I find it gratifying in the extreme, Ozzy, that some things never change. You're still chattering nineteen to the dozen, and woe betide anyone who dares to attempt to slide a word in edgewise." Seating himself across the table from his friend, he took up the bottle the servant wench had brought and drank from it, saying, "Best order another for yourself, old man, as I've got plans for this one."

"Girl!" Ozzy bellowed, thinking Kit was out to make a night of it and more than willing to match him drink for drink. "Bring a bottle. Bring a dozen bottles! Eh? Oh, yes, Kit, of course. And two glasses, you silly chit; what kind of heathens do you think you've got here?"

Three hours and more than a half-dozen bottles later, Kit and Ozzy were still sitting at the table, their reminiscences of the Peninsula having brought tears as well as smiles as their thoughts passed over events past and friends lost, and they were at last ready to speak about the present.

"Earl of Bourne, is it?" Ozzy repeated, clearly pleased for his old friend. "Well, if that don't beat the Dutch. And there you were hobnobbing around the muck of Spain like the rest of us, just as if you was ordinary folk. Why ain't you rubbing shoulders with the rest of the nobs at White's or Boodle's, instead of this low life at the bottom of St. James's?"

"Oh, cut line, Ozzy. You belong to both those clubs, and Almack's to boot, as I remember your tales of that woeful excuse for a select gathering spot for the *haut ton* and the ugly ducklings your mama forced you to bear-lead around the floor."

"Snicker all you wish, you cynic," Ozzy shot back, thinking to trump Kit's ace, "but you'll soon be hounding me to get you a voucher—need one, you know, if you're on the hangout for a wife. Stands to reason you'll be wanting to settle down now that you're a blinkin' earl."

Kit drank deep from his glass. "I'll take you up on that offer of securing a voucher, but I have to tell you, friend, I have been nothing if not thorough since last we met. Within a week of hitting these shores—having happily put those months of convalescence in Portugal behind me—I acquired a title, a large estate, a, I must say, considerable fortune, *and* a wife."

Ozzy sat up straight in his chair, knocking his half-full glass over into his lap in the process. "Ain't you the downy one! How could you get yourself tied up so fast? It's not like you was hanging out for a wife so soon—no rich young bachelor would be so dense as to forgo the joy of wading through the debutantes for at least one Season on the town. Tell you what, you were in your cups—or suffering from some lingering fever caused by your wound. I'm right, aren't I? Say I'm right, Kit, and then tell me her name. Is she pretty?"

"Put a muzzle on it, Ozzy," Kit implored, his head beginning to reflect the combined assault of drink and his friend's garrulous tongue. "Her name is Jane Maitland, and her father's land runs alongside my estate."

"Greedy bugger, ain't you?" slipped in Mr. Norwood, earning himself a hard stare from the earl, who had hoped to find more sympathy from his oldest and best friend.

"That's an insult, Ozzy, damned if it ain't," the new earl declared, slurring his words only slightly. "Damned if I won't cut you dead when next we meet. Besides, Jennie's a charming enough nitwit; I might have pursued her anyway, without her father threatening revenge if I didn't do right by her."

"You did *wrong* by her? And who's Jennie? Thought you said her name was Jane." Clearly Ozzy was perplexed. "You know, Kit, sometimes you don't make a whole lot of sense."

"I've been known to have that reputation," Kit said ruefully. "Ozzy," he continued, leaning forward across the table confidingly, "I need your word of honor that this goes no further."

"Word of a gentleman!" Ozzy swore, then hic-
cupped. "I'll be quiet as a tomb, I swear it." He
leaned forward to put his nose smack against
Kit's. "Spill your guts, my friend, Ozzy's here."

And so, as the dusk gave way to darkness, and
before drunkenness turned to near insensibility,
Kit told his tale to his awestruck audience.

When the story was done and Ozzy had commiserated with his friend's ill luck, the question
was raised: "And what are you going to do about
the chit? Can't wish her gone, can't do her in, not
without the father kicking up a fuss."

"Do with her?" Kit repeated, concentrating on
the mighty task of directing his hand in the
general direction of the bottle before him. "I don't
see that I have to do anything with her. After all,
Ozzy, how much trouble can one small female
be?"

For the next week, Kit was conspicuous in Berkeley Square only by his absence—a fact Jennie
duly took note of, sent up fervent thanks for, and
secretly credited to her masterful handling of
that single interview the day following their hasty
marriage. Sure that her parting shot had put her
firmly in the position of power—with the tenor
and direction of their marriage to be dictated
solely by her—she felt she had left the earl with
no option but to cool his heels while she became
"more comfortable" with their delicate situation.

And she had been immensely "comfortable" in
his absence, as Kit had seemed to abandon even
his halfhearted suggestion that they get to know
one another better. If the truth be told, there
were times Jennie almost forgot she was married
at all, pretending instead that she was in town
for the come-out her father had promised, then

conveniently forgotten to deliver. If only Renfrew
would refrain from calling her "my lady" every
time she so much as passed in the hallway. And
if Bundy would only cease her endless sermons
on the behavior befitting a countess (and the
folly of thinking one could play with fire without
being burned—as if Jennie's inadvertent compro-
mise was the act of a misbehaving child with Kit
cast in the role of a highly combustible match).
And if only Goldie would stop dropping into a
comical knee-cracking curtsy each time Jennie
looked her way—which had driven Jennie to walking about with her eyes averted in some other
direction, leading to more than a few stubbed
toes and bruised shins.

But her companions as well as the facts were
against her. Only Kit, by his absence, gave her
any respite, and at times she could almost find it
in her heart to be in charity with the man. Almost, but not quite. After all, if not for his, as
Bundy called them, "male urges," she'd still be at
home, dreaming safe dreams about the handsome knight on a white charger who would rescue her from the fire-breathing dragon and carry
her off to his castle, where they would live happily ever after.

But even though he was seldom seen, the earl's
presence in Berkeley Square could not be denied.
Every day after rising at the heathen hour of
eleven, Kit breakfasted in his rooms, allowed
himself to be dressed by Leon, who was still
determined to turn a perfectly presentable Corinthian into a dashing darling of fashion, and exited
the mansion, his departing form variously disappearing around the corner of the square on foot,
vaulting into the seat of his new curricle and
giving his horses the office to start, or bending

himself into the smart town carriage that then bore
him off in the regal style befitting his station—
always with Jennie discreetly watching his leave-
takings from behind her curtained window, happily waving him on his way. Where he went did
not concern her. She was only grateful to have
him gone.

Renfrew, on the other hand, had a pretty good
idea of just what his lordship's travels encom-
passed. Struts down Bond Street on the arms of
his cronies, tours through an assortment of low
taverns, forays into the world of ivory turners
and cardsharps at seamy private gaming hells,
hours spent in the blue room at Covent Garden
negotiating an opera dancer's current asking price
for her oft-sold virtue, and an innocent prank or
two aimed at livening the watch's dull existence
would all number among the earl's activities,
unless things had changed mightily since Renfrew
was last in London town.

Natural high spirits and the thrill of being
reunited with his boyhood friends might have
explained this earnest pursuit of pleasure that
nightly had Kit beating the rising sun home by
less than an hour, but Renfrew knew there was
another, deeper reason.

It was the dream. The dream that sent Renfrew
scurrying from his warm bed on the first night of
the new earl's residence at Bourne Manor, the
wicked, panic-filled dreams that tore ragged moans
and hoarse screams from the sleeping man's throat
until Leon's soothing voice could penetrate the
panic and lull the tormented earl back to sleep.

Leon either did not know or would not divulge
the nature of the recurring nightmare that had
the earl calling the name Denny over and over
again, the memory whose nocturnal reenactment

moved the man to dry sobs and broken pleas for help.

The dream seemed to have disappeared, the last nightmare occurring the night before the earl's marriage, but Renfrew knew it wasn't so. The earl was fighting the nightmare in the only way he knew—by not falling into bed until he was either too exhausted or too deep in his cups to dream at all.

The old butler, who had served the Wilde family man and boy, could only stand back and let his master battle with his private demons, knowing the outcome but not daring to overstep his place by telling his lordship he was fighting a losing battle.

Renfrew could only watch and hope, believing the gentle child he had watched grow into the giving, compassionate young woman the earl had married was the only key to the man's salvation. Yet Jennie and Kit might as well have been residing on separate continents for all they saw of each other. It was enough to make a stronger man than Renfrew despair. But not Renfrew—he only bided his time while making plans of his own.

As part of his project designed to invest Jennie with some passionate feelings for this particular Bourne domicile and her position as mistress of all it contained, Renfrew spent three full days acquainting her with every stick of furniture in every room of the mansion, impressing her with the history of this original painting and that priceless set of engraved silver plate.

His efforts were not in vain. Jennie was not impressed by the wealth spread out before her, but rather with the stories of the Bourne ancestors who had furnished the mansion with such care and love. That the responsibility for maintaining the beauty around her as well as placing this generation's personal stamp on the place by way of worthy additions of art and other accessories that would reflect their times while not detracting from what had gone before was now hers was not lost on Jennie. It surprised her, though, to realize that she was more than eager to take up the challenge.

The more mundane side of running a household, neatly catalogued in a half-dozen closely written ledgers, did not inspire the same creative urges. In fact, after pretending a studious perusal of just two of the big black leather-bound books, Jennie pleaded a headache and Renfrew kindly moved the dratted things out of her sight.

"Renfrew," Jennie proposed, once the butler had poured her a bracing cup of tea, "I'd like to strike a bargain with you. If you will consent to managing the household accounts, acting as secretary or whatever, I shall, besides offering you my eternal gratitude, undertake the hiring of the additional staff his lordship tells me we require."

Happy to see her showing such an interest, such a willingness to involve herself, no matter how indirectly, with his lordship's comfort, Renfrew agreed with alacrity. After all, he told himself airily, what could go wrong in the mere hiring of household staff?

And with that thought Renfrew proved yet again that, be he earl or butler, a male is still a male—never failing to underestimate the tremendous potential for disruption that churns just beneath the surface of those apparently fragile feminine forms men so condescendingly refer to as the weaker sex.

*   *   *

There was a great deal of perverse satisfaction to be derived from flouting your husband's wishes, Jennie learned as she and Goldie climbed back into the town carriage after concluding her business with the clerk in charge of placing advertisements in the *Observer*.

She was pleased with the wording of her advertisement—certainly the clerk had seen no reason to change so much as the placement of a single comma—and she rode home secure in the belief that this more personal form of advertising would result in bringing to her door a fair number of robust, hardworking country folk who were new to London and eager for honest work they could not find due to lack of references.

That's what she wanted. Country folk. Plump, red-cheeked farm girls and strong, raw-boned farmers' sons who'd remind her of home. After all, what did she want with a passel of top-lofty London servants who were known far and wide for aping their masters while at the same time despising the very people who paid their wages?

She had done the right thing, she was sure of it. The fact that she had planned her trip to the newspaper office to coincide with Bundy's monthly retreat to her couch due to a regular-as-clockwork migraine headache proved nothing to the contrary, absolutely nothing.

As they rode along the crowded street, Jennie rechecked her list. Heading it was the need for a chef—Renfrew had informed her that Kit had specifically requested a French chef—followed by notations calling for three additional footmen, two kitchen helpers, a pair of experienced stable hands, at least two more housemaids who could double at serving table, and, perhaps even a tweeny to run errands between floors if she could find one.

It seemed ostentatious to require nearly two dozen people to care for the needs and comforts of a family consisting of two young, healthy creatures who by all rights should be capable of fending for themselves.

Of course, they weren't two *average* people, she amended mentally. After all, how many English couples live in eighteen-room houses containing a conservatory, two separate dining rooms, and a veritable barn of a ballroom? Bundy said the Bourne mansion was no more than a fit setting for an earl and his countess. Jennie wisely refrained from wondering aloud if this particular earl and countess didn't look just a tad out of place in their grand surroundings—almost like children playing at being all grown up.

Kit, she had to admit, at least looked the part, having visited his tailor before traveling to Bourne Manor so that an entire new wardrobe had been waiting for him in Berkeley Square, but she knew her own simple gowns to be sadly provincial. Which was why the Bourne carriage was just then coming to a halt outside a fashionable shop in Bond Street (this part of her trip also deliberately planned around Bundy's migraine or else Jennie knew she'd be the first countess in history to be dressed entirely in concealing white dimity gowns matched to sensible, serviceable jean boots).

Goldie was in her glory as she stood gaping and gawking throughout Jennie's lengthy session with the modiste. A young woman of definite tastes that had previously taken second place to her budget, Jennie worked her way purposefully from one end of the selling room to the other, selecting lengths of material with an eye

to color and texture and never once bothering to
ask a single price.

In the space of an hour Jennie had matched
the materials to sketches the delighted modiste
swore on her hopes of heaven were designed with
just madam countess in mind. "That exquisite
waist! That so entrancing swell of bosom—so innocent, so alluring! The regal carriage of a princess, the fine molded arms of a Greek goddess.
The hair of an angel, the skin of a newborn babe.
Ooh la la! That the countess would deign to honor
this humble establishment with her attention. It
will be the making of a poor, struggling widow in
a foreign land. Once madam is seen in public the
ton will demand a like transformation—an impossible task, to duplicat', such beauty, my lady,
but one must make a living." On and on went the
modiste.

Two hours after entering the shop, Jennie departed, her head still buzzing with the French-
woman's ridiculous compliments and fervent ex-
pressions of gratitude (the latter being more
readily believed if Jennie had but known the
total of the bill). She changed her mind about
shopping for shoes, bonnets, gloves, and other
accessories, putting off that errand for another
day even if it meant she must listen to Bundy's
prudish criticisms of her every choice. She had a
headache of her very own now, the result of the
modiste's incessant chatter and a growing hun-
ger for her lunch, which may have accounted for
her almost violent reaction to seeing her husband
strolling down the opposite side of the street, a
soft, clinging bit of frailty hanging from each
elbow.

It was ridiculous. Why should she feel this almost overpowering urge to dash across the street

and plummet the two slyly simpering creatures
about the head and shoulders with her reticule?
And when she had done with them she would
deliver a bash or five on the noggin of the stupidly grinning ignoramus who was acting less
like a married man than Prinny himself!

She stood stock still on the flagway, rooted to
the spot by her anger and her inability to do
more than mentally mangle the cause of her upset.

"*O-oo-o,* lookee, miss," Goldie piped up loudly
at exactly the wrong moment. "There's his lordship himself, out for a breath of air. *Yoo-hoo!
Your lordship!*" she trilled in a high, carrying
soprano, her voice succeeding in reaching the
earl above the noisy street sounds and the animated chattering of his companions.

"Oh, my *God!*" Kit breathed in exasperation as
he spied Goldie and his wife—his oddly *erect*
wife—on the opposite side of the street. What a
coil! He couldn't abandon the two females on the
crowded flagway, and he wasn't such a gapeseed
as to drag them with him and introduce them to
his wife of seven days. Yet to ignore his wife
entirely was courting disaster. Besides, that dratted maid would probably keep bellowing like a
sick calf until he acknowledged their presence.
He was damned no matter what he did!

And then Lady Luck, in the form of one Oswald
Norwood, came sauntering toward him, and Kit
began to believe in good fairies. "Ozzy, my dearest
friend," he intoned bravely, "would you be so
kind as to escort these ladies to a hackney? I'm
afraid I've forgotten an urgent appointment."

Ozzy was delighted, a fact Kit did not linger to
learn, hurrying instead across the street, neatly
dodging horses and vehicles that dared to get in
his path, to stand smartly, and just a bit breath-

lessly, in a direct line between his wife and his too recent companions. "I did not know you had planned to visit the shops, my dear," he said with studied nonchalance.

Jennie leaned a bit to the left and peered over his shoulder at the females, who still stood where Kit had left them. "Obviously," she drawled sweetly, "else you would have asked me to join your party. Wouldn't you?"

Wretched chit! he swore silently, acting just as if we had vowed fidelity or some such rot. Which they had! he remembered with a jolt. "Party?" he improvised rapidly. "Oh, pet, you mistake the facts entirely. Those young ladies are—er—cousins of my friend Ozzy, the man with them now. I was just lending them my company while he dashed off a moment to speak with an acquaintance he hadn't seen for some time. Merely holding the fort, as it were," he ended with a limp laugh.

"Really?" Jennie's voice conveyed her disbelief. "It's a shame they had to rush off without so much as an introduction. But perhaps we can have them to dinner one evening. We know so few people in London, you know." It was amazing how calm her voice sounded, considering she was still seriously contemplating homicide.

"Yes, well, er, you shouldn't let the horses stand too much longer, Jennie," Kit said in sudden inspiration. "Allow me to escort you home, and, er, we can take luncheon together. I've been so busy establishing my bona fides at the banks and seeking out friends from my army days that I'm guilty of neglecting you, aren't I, puss? I confess to feeling ashamed."

You could charm the pennies off a dead man's eyes, Jennie decided nastily, hating herself for feeling her outrage slowly melting under Kit's

engagingly open grin. Now her anger was somehow redirecting itself, turning away from her
husband and centering on her own overreaction
to seeing him in the company of two, she reluctantly acknowledged, beautiful females, when she
herself didn't care two sticks for the man personally. In fact, had Kit only promptly shepherded
his wife into the coach he might have come out of
the whole episode with nary a scratch, so angry
was Jennie with herself. But Lady Luck had deserted him too soon this sunny spring day and
the storm clouds were gathering, soon to rain all
over his victory.

"Kit," came the voice of Ozzy Norwood as he
joined his friend after sending two very disgruntled ladies on their way back to Drury Lane. "I
demand you return my favor and introduce me to
your beautiful companion. Two for one may not
be a fair exchange, but then a simple mister
cannot command the same privileges as an earl,
what? By the by," he added, securing his friend's
coffin with a few finishing nails, "this one makes
those two warblers look like yesterday's kippers,
stap me if they don't. Can't blame you for dump-
ing them in my lap and loping off like that."

A large rock—possibly Gibraltar itself—was
lodged in Lord Bourne's throat, making coherent
speech impossible, although he did try a time or
two, gasping and choking badly before subsiding
into silence and glaring at his grinning friend.

Just as Ozzy's eyes were belatedly taking in
Jennie's simple but well-cut gown and the presence of a female much resembling a lady's maid
standing in front of what looked suspiciously like
Bourne's town carriage—a small glimmer of light
beginning to grow in his pleasantly vacant face—
Jennie stepped into the breach and took charge.

Extending a small gloved hand in his direction, she said brightly, "You must be one of my husband's good friends—one of those selfish creatures who so monopolize his time in lengthy sessions reminiscing about your shared youths. But I'll forgive your interruption of our honeymoon, as I know how greatly Kit enjoys reliving his childish exploits. He must, mustn't he, as I have not seen him above a moment or two since we arrived in town."

"It's all my fault!" Ozzy sacrificed bravely. "He didn't want to be with us, you know. We fairly *begged* for his company. Don't blame him, my lady, I implore you—"

Jennie pretended to pout, throwing out her full bottom lip, thereby nearly inciting her husband to violence, then brightened visibly as she said, "I have it! You must come to dine. Just as soon as our French chef is in residence—say, a week from today? And bring your two cousins, as I do so pine for some female companionship. After all, sir, any friend of Kit's cannot help but find welcome in Berkeley Square. Isn't that so, dear?" she asked the mute earl. Was that smoke she saw coming out of her husband's ears? she thought, feeling rather full of herself.

"You're kind, ma'am," Ozzy blustered, his overtaxed intellect reeling under the barrage his *faux pas* had unleashed and powerless to maneuver out of range of attack. "Too—*too*—kind. Indeed," he said, attempting an air of worldliness, "Kit is undeserving of such a fine lady as yourself."

"Why thank you, sir," Jennie responded. "I quite agree. But then we so seldom get what we deserve, don't we?"

At last Kit found his tongue. "Oh, I don't know about that, my love," he put in, leading her toward the open door of the coach. "Some of us get *exactly* what we deserve. In fact, one of us might just get it this very night if she continues asking for it so blatantly."

"Really?" Jennie exclaimed, bravado masking the fact that her knees were beginning to experience a decided tendency to quiver. In a much lower voice heard only by her husband she added, "My papa always warned me that people who choose to live in glass houses should beware of tossing rocks. Look to yourself, my *love*, before casting any stones at *my* behavior. Retribution can be demanded on both sides."

After delivering this stunning *coup de grace,* Jennie turned, inclined her head to her husband's friend and incidental tattletale, and allowed herself to be assisted into the carriage. Blond head held high, she concentrated on her second verbal victory over her husband and determinedly resisted any thoughts concerning her ridiculous overreaction upon seeing Kit enjoying the company of any female besides his wife—who wouldn't cross the street with him if he asked her to, which, she owned sourly, he hadn't.

As the carriage drove away Kit turned to his lifelong friend, ready to do murder in broad daylight while standing in the middle of crowded Bond Street. "Now, now, Kit, old chum, it was an honest mistake," Ozzy began, hastily backing up a step. "You never told me your wife was such a looker. Anyway, wives ain't supposed to be pretty. They're supposed to have big dowries and buck teeth. And hatchet noses. And ... and ... and scrawny chests—"

"Keep your filthy mouth off my wife's chest!" Kit was so overcome as to bluster before realizing exactly what he was saying. "Never mind that! What in thunder did you think you were about, prancing over here like some hound in heat and cadging a tryst with my wife as if she were some trollop we'd share between us? Are your brains entirely to let that you'd mistake a lady for one of your loose women? I ought to call you out for this, Ozzy, I swear it!"

Ozzy cast his eyes about furtively and spoke out of the side of his mouth. "Attracting a crowd, sport. What say we toddle down to White's and settle this quietly over a bottle? My treat, o' course. Call me out, you say. You wouldn't really do that, Kit, would you? Deuced unsporting of you, knowing what a fine shot you are, don't you think?"

Looking around, Kit reluctantly realized the wisdom of Ozzy's warning—while hating to credit his friend with even a small portion of brainpower at that moment—and roughly grabbing the fellow by the elbow, he surreptitiously pushed him along the flagway as if unsure Ozzy wouldn't bolt if he relaxed his hold.

It took more than one bottle before Kit could find any small bit of humor in the scene lately enacted in Bond Street, but no amount of wine or conciliating chatter on the part of Ozzy would make Kit believe Jennie could be induced to speak to him again much before the first snow of winter.

Chapter Five

For a man who had so distinguished himself in battle as to have been mentioned in dispatches more than a half-dozen times, Kit showed a remarkable lack of courage when it came to confronting his wife. Perhaps this reluctance to face her stemmed from the fact that he knew himself to be totally in the wrong—as even the slapdash marital habits of the *ton* included at least a show of fidelity, certainly during the first flush of the union.

So Jennie was left to wade her way through the long list of applicants who replied to her advertisement—their numbers making a long, snaking line that stretched from the servants' entrance into Berkeley Square itself—while the earl continued making himself scarce.

Five days after their meeting on Bond Street, Kit at last ran out of diversions and found himself, at only three in the afternoon, at loose ends. Lacking any other alternative, he directed his mount to the rear of Berkeley Square, dismounted in front of the stable doors, turned, and walked headfirst into a mountain.

"What the devil?" Bourne exploded once he had regained his breath. Looking up, quite a good way up, actually, his startled eyes took in the sight of an enormous, hairless, black head

fitted with glittering black-bean eyes; a gargantuan head that sat atop the largest man Kit had
ever seen.

Two hands as large as hams reached out to
steady him, nearly crushing his shoulders in the
process, as Kit rocked slightly on his heels. The
man must be all of seven feet tall, the gaping
earl told himself in amazement. *I can only hope
he's a friendly beast.*

Recovering his dignity and firmly stamping
down any impulse to turn tail and make a run
for it, Kit inquired softly: "What—er, I mean,
who are you?"

"I be called Tiny," the giant rumbled from somewhere deep in his massive chest.

"Naturally," the earl quipped ruefully, his quick
sense of the ridiculous coming to the rescue.

"I be the earl's new groom. Who be you, sir?"

"I be—er—I'm the earl, actually," Kit informed
him, stepping out of Tiny's large shadow and
back into the sunlight. "So, you're my new groom,
eh, Tiny? Tell me—who hired you?" Kit held out
a hand before Tiny could answer. "No, don't tell
me, let me guess. Lady Bourne, right?"

"Lady Bourne, she be a queen. I be ready to die
for her," Tiny growled passionately. "I be ready
to kill for her. With these hands," he swore, holding out his large fists and then clenching them
tight.

Kit swallowed hard and stretched his neck.
"Good, Tiny. I like—um—*loyalty* in a servant.
But I asked her ladyship to secure two grooms."
He looked the giant up and down, still amazed by
the man's size. "Or did she think she had?"

"'ullo, guv'nor," came a thin, high voice as
Tiny stepped sideways to reveal the person stand-

ing behind him. "Goliath's m'name and groomin' nags m'game. Me an' Tiny 'ere 're a team, ye ken. Worked the travelin' circus till it went flat, an' yer missus took us up. Right pretty piece too," Goliath added with a wink, earning himself a menacing growl from Tiny.

"A dwarf," Kit breathed in amazement, looking down on the tiny man. "A bloody dwarf." And then, remarkably, he grinned. "Why not? Why the bloody hell not?"

"You be wantin' Tiny ta take yer horse?" the large man asked almost timidly, belatedly remembering his mistress's hint that the earl was best humored at first, until he felt more at ease with his new staff.

"That's very kind of you, Tiny," Kit thanked the man as he turned and headed toward the rear of the mansion. "Just toss him over your shoulder, why not, and carry him into his stall. I'm sure he'll give you no trouble."

Goliath let out a giggle and executed a perfect, if compact, backflip. " 'e likes us, Tiny," the delighted dwarf crowed, jumping up and down on his sturdy, stubby legs. " 'ome at last we is, boyo, 'ome at last!"

Jennie paced the drawing room in mounting apprehension. Kit's behavior had been courtesy itself since their unfortunate meeting in Bond Street, not only refraining from taking out his threatened revenge on her person, but allowing time and distance to separate them from the nastier memories of that meeting.

Since she had spent a very busy week interviewing possible servants for the mansion, Jennie's memories of that fateful meeting had been given a chance to mellow, so that now she could recall little of her former anger, concentrating instead on the ludicrous image of her infuriatingly urbane husband at a total loss for words. Of her other, more unsettling feelings at having spied two obvious ladies of the evening dangling from her husband's sleeves, she refused to think at all. It only confused the issue, whatever it was.

She'd been granted time, and time was what she had needed. Time to complete her new wardrobe, and time for some of her new things to be delivered, so that she could, when the time came, face him in her new finery. That was important. She needed the outward trappings of her new title about her when her husband confronted her demanding she explain about the servants she had hired.

Oh, yes, she mused knowingly, there would be quite a grand to-do then. She was not a complete fool. But she must make him understand her reasons for hiring Tizzie and Lizzie, Tiny and Goliath, Charity—the poor, dear thing—Bob, Ben, and Del, and Irvette and Blessing. Even Montague, the French chef Kit had particularly requested, would require a good deal of explaining on her part, she knew.

Now the time and space Kit had granted her began to wear on her nerves. She yearned to have him summon her, ring a peal over her head, and have done with it.

Bundy had told her he would. Even Goldie had clucked her tongue at the sight of Charity—the poor, dear thing. Renfrew, Jennie silently blessed the man, had said nothing, possibly because Del's happy "Mornin', guv'nor" as he took up his proper footman position in the foyer had robbed the majordomo of coherent speech.

Deep in her heart of hearts, Jennie knew she had grossly overstepped herself. She had been commissioned to hire the servants, of course she had been, but she had not been given *carte blanche* to employ the odd assortment of humanity she had chosen. But they had needed jobs so desperately, she consoled herself. All those other, qualified applicants, who had presented themselves, references in hand, would have no difficulty in finding positions.

But Tizzie and Lizzie, for instance, had little hope if she turned them down. Where could two overage, out-of-work Shakespearean actresses find work if even the lowest traveling troupe would not hire them? And as for Charity—the poor, dear thing—she might well expire in a filthy gutter if Jennie hadn't taken her on as tweeny. Not that Charity could climb the stairs very much in her present condition.

Surely Kit would understand. Jennie picked up a Dresden statuette of a young maiden and scowled into its placid, peaceful face. And a herd of elephants might dance on the head of a pin. Of course Kit wouldn't understand! Why should he? Hadn't the man already proved himself to be a heartless beast capable of compromising an innocent maiden, marrying her, and then deserting her in the midst of a strange city?

Jennie rapidly worked up a full head of steam, all her heat directed at her cruel husband, the heartless monster from whom she must protect her latest batch of ugly ducklings and pitiful misfits. How dare he question her judgment! Who was he to set himself up as arbiter of all that was required to make a good and loyal servant? Well, she thought, now in a high state of temper, just let him say one word against her choices. Just let him dare!

Kit's entrance into the drawing room at that precise moment was not exactly a triumph of superb timing. "Good day, m'love," he began cheerily enough. "And what are you about today?"

Jennie whirled on him in some heat. "And just what is *that* snide remark supposed to mean?" she sneered, her green eyes narrowed into wary slits. "How unhandsome of you, Kit, how very unhandsome of you!"

"I make you my compliments, ma'am," Kit drawled, executing an elegant leg in her direction. "That is quite a novel greeting. Am I, I sincerely trust, going to be given an explanation for it, or am I to be summarily executed for my sins without even so much as a hearing?"

Jennie tossed her blond curls and sniffed. "Oh, you think you're so very droll, don't you?"

She ain't exactly falling over herself to be nice to me, Kit told himself, hiding a smile. Possibly she feels attack to be the best defense. I wonder what she believes herself to be guilty of, for I doubt I have been in Berkeley Square frequently enough to have done anything too lamentable. "What is it, puss?" he prompted, lowering his rangy frame into a chair and stretching his legs before him. "Have you overspent your allowance? If so, don't fret, for if that fetching creation you are wearing is part of the reason I forgive you with all my heart. You really do clean up quite nicely, pet, if I must say so m'self."

Having successfully taken himself out of the pan and placed himself squarely in the fire, Kit subsided into silence, content to watch the sparks now emanating from his wife's eyes.

Plopping down on the settee opposite his chair,

Jennie spat nastily, "Oh, do be quiet. I know very well you have just come from the stables, dressed as you are. Don't tell me you don't have something cutting to say to me about our new grooms, for it won't fadge, Kit, truly it won't. Well," she nudged, "go on—have done with it. Tell me I am the greatest fool since time began— even Bundy would not gainsay you."

Kit had the audacity to assume a crestfallen expression. "How low your opinion is of me, ma'am. I had nary a thought but to praise you on your finds. What splendid grooms Tiny and Goliath will make. Goliath can tend horsey hoofs all the day long without ever complaining of a sore back, and Tiny—why, the man is invaluable. If one of my blacks comes up lame I've simply to set Tiny between the shafts and I'll have the fastest curricle in all London, possibly all England."

"Don't you make fun of them," Jennie shot at him angrily. "Don't you dare make fun of them!"

The smile left Kit's handsome face. "I do not make fun of them, Jennie. It is you who demean them by thinking they are in need of your protection. It is you who sees them as different, not me. Oh, I admit to being momentarily startled by their rather, er, different *appearance*, but I believe I recovered in time so as to not embarrass either them or myself." He leaned back and crossed his legs at the ankle. "Actually, pet, it is you who should be apologizing to me for believing I would let some sort of prejudice against people who are a bit different influence my consideration of their talents. If they prove to be good grooms, they shall stay. If not"—his voice hardened fractionally—"no power on earth will induce me to keep them on. Do we understand each other?"

Jennie had the good grace to feel ashamed of herself and said so—quite prettily—causing Kit's smile to return. It was then, as she was enjoying this show of friendly compatibility, that she decided to press her luck.

"Tiny and Goliath are not the only servants I have hired. You may not be so generous when you have met them."

"Again you malign me before the fact." Kit sighed theatrically. Really, this getting along with wives was not so bad after all. Jennie was proving quite easily maneuverable. She was also, as he had observed earlier, growing to be quite easy on his eyes. Marriage certainly did have its compensations. Hard as it was to believe, he was beginning to truly enjoy her company.

What a pity she was not more worldly or he might be tempted to bed her. Yet, he surprised himself by thinking, he was glad she was not worldly, had little experience of men such as himself. Disturbed by this train of thought, he swiftly turned his mind back to the subject at hand. "Tell me about the rest of our staff, pet. If I am going to live here I guess I should make myself at least tokenly acquainted with them."

Look at him, Jennie told herself irritably, sitting there looking so smug and self-satisfied—and so wretchedly handsome, she added reluctantly. Oh, he thinks he's got me right in the palm of his hand. The high and mighty Earl of Bourne, condescending to be nice to his simple, countrified wife. How dare he try to manipulate me this way! Even worse, how dare he succeed so handily!

She would have verbally taken him to task then, but she could tell, by the disgustingly satisfied smile on his face, that she might just as well save her breath to, as Goldie said, cool her porridge. Well, if he intended to be disobliging she saw no reason not to do likewise. "I see no need to give you a recital of our serving staff, seeing as how you are home so seldom and unlikely to run into other than those on duty after midnight."

So it sits like that, does it, Kit mused, raising one speaking eyebrow as he took in Jennie's flushed cheeks. The kitten has her back up yet again. "I would perceive the wisdom of your words, kitten," he told her with a maddening smile, "except for one thing. I have decided to change my ways, knowing myself to be guilty of shamelessly neglecting you. Dear me," he exclaimed, feigning astonishment as Jennie leaped to her feet and stared down at him open-mouthed, "I do believe I have said something to upset you. Is it the thought of our finally acting the part of man and wife that so discommodes you? Or, might I hope, do I misread your agitation? Perhaps, be still my foolish heart, you too wish for this closer association?"

Jennie stomped away from the settee and took up a position nearer the doorway to the foyer. "There are times, my lord, when you can be unbelievably crude," she said crushingly.

Before Jennie could make good her exit, Kit leaped up from his chair and loped across the room to capture her shoulders in his strong grip. He did not know what imp of mischief had possessed him—surely he had not entered the drawing room with any such thoughts in mind—but suddenly he felt himself overpowered by an undeniable need to feel Jennie's softly pouting mouth beneath his own.

He told himself he was merely kissing her as a means of shutting her up, but he knew he was

lying. The high life he had been living ever since
he came to London had included being in the
company of many beautiful women—women who
neither railed at him nor accused him of every
evil under the sun. No, the women he had spent
time with were all generous females, giving to a
fault—for a price. Yet he had not once sampled
their wares, even though his pockets were now
well lined enough to set up his own stable of fine
fillies. He had flirted, he had teased—but he had
not bedded a one of them.

Jennie, her heart fluttering madly, stared up
into Kit's strangely staring face, unable to know
what was going on in his mind. If she knew that
the thought of a small, blond slip of an unwanted
bride had kept her dashing husband celibate she
would not have believed it. That was probably
why, although he looked about to speak, her husband said nothing. He only continued to stare—
taking his own sweet time about it too.

As the tension in the air became nearly thick
enough to slice, he acted. Abruptly dragging her
soft body up against his lean, hard frame, Kit
swooped like a bird of prey and claimed Jennie's
unsuspecting mouth in a nearly ruthless kiss.

The flash of feeling was instant and just as
intense as he remembered. Almost at once his
lips softened, moving sensuously as they molded
themselves to the warm contours of Jennie's. He
felt the heat rising within him as he pressed his
body more firmly against her yielding form, and
his heart leaped at the very moment he felt the
tenseness leave her and her hands begin to inch
up to clasp his waist.

As for Jennie, she wasn't thinking at all. She
was leagues past rational thought and had been
from the moment she was first rudely captured

in Kit's arms. Try as she might to tell herself it was fear that held her captive, she knew she was only deceiving herself. She wanted Kit to touch her, to kiss her. Perhaps she had subconsciously been hoping for just such a reaction when she had insulted him. This and a lot more she would sit alone in her room and dissect later. Much later. Right now she would give in to the enjoyment of the moment.

But all good things must come to an end, and this interlude was no exception. Why he looked up he did not know; perhaps a noise distracted him—although he found it hard to believe anything could have distracted him, so intense was his concentration on the logistics of transferring their activity from the doorway to the settee— but suddenly his eyes were taking in the sight of a small, mobcapped servant girl surreptitiously crossing the foyer.

"Bloody hell!" he exclaimed, releasing Jennie so abruptly she nearly fell. "That chit's *pregnant!*"

Jennie shook her head a time or two, trying hard to bring herself back to reality. "Increasing," she corrected at last, striving for a bit of dignity. "Charity—the poor, dear thing—will be presenting us with a little bundle of joy in about a month."

"In a pig's eye she will!" the earl countered hotly. "It's not a home for fallen women I'm running here, damn it all." All thoughts of shared passion forgotten, Kit rounded on Jennie and ordered coldly, "Get rid of her. Now! Today!"

Her hands planted firmly on her hips, her head and shoulders leaning toward him for emphasis, Jennie responded, "Charity is my choice for tweeny. You said I could have one if I wished.

Well, I wish. I shall pay her wages out of my own
allowance if necessary, but I promised that child
a home, and a home she shall have!"

Kit lifted a hand to his pounding head. "Who's
the father? Do we employ him as well?"

Now Jennie was in her element. "We do not,
my lord. The father is a peer of the realm, already married and father to more children than
Adam. He seduced poor Charity within a month
of her employment in Grosvenor Sq—"

"Spare me his name, infant," Kit cut in resign-
edly, "else you may yet tell me it is my duty to
call the cad out to avenge the chit." Reluctantly
nodding his head in surrender he sighed, "All
right, Jennie. Charity, as they say, begins at
home. I guess our home is as good a place as any.
But for the sake of our unnamed peer, I suggest
you keep Charity abovestairs until after her
confinement."

"You are not going to fight me on this?" Jennie
asked incredulously, finding it hard to accept
this easy victory.

"I be fond of my own skin, I be," the earl
quipped in imitation of Tiny's peculiar phrasing,
"and I be leery of your setting your great giant
after me if I refuse."

Kit's magnanimity, as well as the lingering
softness she felt for him after their embrace, combined to put a smile back on Jennie's face. "Should
I spare you more surprises and tell you about the
rest of the staff?"

The Earl of Bourne, that so beset and belea-
guered man, merely shook his head in denial. "In
consideration of my sanity, pet, I believe you
should refrain from such an inventory and leave
me to discover them one at a time. Although I

cannot imagine that anything can surprise me anymore." Turning to quit the room, he added one last thought. "Other females content themselves collecting bric-a-brac, y'know. But I guess that would be too tame a hobby for you, wouldn't it, kitten?"

He left then, taking her furious blush as his answer, and went in search of his valet and a hot tub, leaving Jennie alone in the drawing room to relive his kiss and her daring response to it.

"Tonight, my infant," he whispered under his breath as he climbed the wide stairs. "Tonight we will resume what Charity, that 'poor, dear thing' you have taken under your wing, interrupted. It is more than time I began acting the husband."

The headache that had been the excuse Jennie offered in order to get out of dining with her husband that evening became a reality a few hours later. Pacing alone in her bedchamber (having effectively banished Bundy and Goldie with her tearful pleas to be left alone in her misery), Jennie's abused head rang with her companions' parting words that echoed over and over in her ears: "You'll have to face up to your actions sooner or later, missy."

Jennie tossed her head arrogantly as she tried to dismiss Bundy's words. "No, I don't," she denied aloud. "I can go home to Papa and never set foot in London again." Her triumphant grin faded abruptly as she realized her title-conscious father would send her back to London so fast her feet wouldn't touch the ground.

"I can take refuge in a convent," she announced to the empty room, then made a face as she realized the absurdity of such a move. "Well, what else can I do?" she asked her reflection in the full-length mirror. "I can't very well disguise myself as a man and ship out on some vessel bound for India. I get seasick on the pond at home." She leaned her forehead against the cool glass. "Maybe I'll just hide away in here until I go into a decline and Kit loses interest." She raised her head slightly to look into her own eyes. "Oh, fudge!" she exclaimed pettishly and turned away from her reflection.

Tossing her dressing gown across a chair, she crawled into bed, pulled the covers over her head, and tried to find peace in a good night's sleep.

Three hours later, still tossing and turning in her rumpled bed, Jennie heard Kit's footsteps climb the stairs and halt outside her door. She held her breath for an eternity of time before his footsteps moved on down the hallway to his own door, then tried to ignore the sound of Kit's voice as Leon helped the earl in his preparations before retiring. It wasn't until the valet could be heard closing the door behind him on his way out that Jennie felt she could relax at last, and it wasn't long until sleep overcame her.

"Denny!" a voice called urgently. "Denny, what happened? Hold on! I'm coming!" Jennie sat straight up in bed, eyes wide with fright, her heart pounding in her chest. Someone had called her name. "Denny! Oh no, Denny!" the masculine voice cried yet again, torment in every syllable.

It wasn't her name that was being called, Jennie realized. It just sounded like it to her sleep-fuzzed mind. Her bare toes hit the floor as she involuntarily responded to the anguish in Kit's voice—for she could tell it was her husband who was calling out, probably in the throes of a nightmare—and, being Jennie, she had no other thought but to go to him and comfort him, her dressing gown left behind forgotten on the chair.

Swinging open the connecting door between their chambers, the door that had remained firmly closed all the time they had resided in Berkeley Square, she stumbled through the dim light cast by the full moon out that night and made her way to the side of the large bed. Fumbling with the familiar implements, she at last lit the candle next to Kit's bed, and her husband's face came into view—a face ravaged with some pain that twisted his features and drove his clenched fists into the mattress on either side of his body.

She reached out her hands and shook his shoulders. "Kit. Kit!" she whispered loudly. "Kit, wake up. You're having a nightmare." But Kit was too far away to hear her, his mind locked in some hellish place her voice could not reach. Again, Jennie didn't think; again, she acted. She crawled into the bed and put her arms around his thrashing body, pressing her cheek next to his, and began to croon softly, as one would to a distraught child.

"Denny!" Kit breathed, seeming to quiet a bit. "I knew I could find you. The cannon—where did they all come from? Ambush, Denny, caught napping." Kit's hands reached up and clamped themselves around Jennie's slim form. "So much blood, Denny. Ah, my side. It hurts like hell. Where's Denny? He was next to me when the ball hit. Denny?" Kit's muscles tightened, and Jennie nearly cried out in pain as his grip punished her soft flesh. *"Denny!"* Kit rasped, the pain in his voice bringing tears to her eyes. "Jesus, Lord, Denny, where are you? *For the love of God, where's the rest of you?"*

"Kit!" Jennie called loudly into his ear, giving his cheek a firm slap as she outwardly strained for control, ignoring her own fear at the sight of his wide, sightlessly staring eyes. "Wake up, my poor darling," she implored on a dry sob. "Please, Kit, wake up!"

She watched anxiously as his eyes blinked once, twice, and then seemed to focus on her face. His hands, crushing her upper arms in their superior strength, relaxed slightly. "It was just a dream, Kit. A nightmare."

Kit's chest was heaving as he struggled to regain control over himself. "Dreaming," he rasped, taking a deep, shuddering breath and letting it out slowly. "Only a dream, only a dream," he parroted, giving his head a slight shake. He reached down somewhere deep inside himself and summoned up a small smile. "And you came to wake me up and chase the bogeymen away. Thank you, kitten."

Leon and Renfrew, standing in the hallway in their nightclothes, exchanged glances and turned away, each returning to his own bed, to think his own thoughts. The valet's hand had been on the doorknob when Renfrew restrained him, shaking his head silently and cocking his head toward the door and mouthing, "Listen." They heard Jennie's voice struggling to be heard over Kit's cries, and both men waited, Leon barely resisting the urge to comfort his friend and master, and Renfrew silently praying that the near strangers on the other side of the heavy wooden door might learn more about each other before this night was over.

Never knowing the two servants had been outside the door, Jennie and Kit, their emotions heightened by the events of the past few minutes, were suddenly tinglingly aware that they were alone in the near dark, lying side by side on a bed, their arms wrapped around each other. When Jennie, in her nervousness, squirmed slightly, the movement brought their bodies even closer together, a fact Kit was not backward in realizing.

"Thank you, kitten," he breathed into her hair. "I must have given you quite a fright."

"Hrummmph, umm-wumpum." Jennie's mouth, pressed firmly against his bare neck, garbled her words, and Kit responded by chuckling deep in his throat. "What was that?" he asked, moving his head away only marginally in order to look into her face.

"I said, 'You're welcome,' " Jennie repeated, flushing hotly under his intense gaze. Pushing against his shoulders with her hands, she tried to rise, mumbling rather incoherently about returning to her own chamber.

"But what if I should have another nightmare?" Kit questioned, using his own hands to push her back down against him. Then, all traces of humor leaving his voice, he asked her softly, "What was I dreaming about, kitten? I never remember much, although I'm fairly certain it's the same dream over and over again. Leon wakes me, my throat raw with screaming, my body drenched in sweat, but I can't remember anything but this— this feeling of terror."

He looked so lost, so vulnerable. Jennie could no more leave him than she could turn away a starving child. Allowing herself to be gathered against his chest, she whispered, "You called for someone named Denny. At first, when you woke me, I thought you were calling my name." As soon as she began speaking, Kit had grown rigid under her, and she knew he was upset. "Who is . . . was . . . Denny? Was he a friend?"

"Lord Denton Lowell. The closest friend, the only friend any one man could ever need or want," Kit told her in a low voice. "He, er, he died on the Peninsula."

Jennie remembered Kit's ramblings about Denny, and a tear formed in the corner of her left eye and splashed onto her husband's silk-clad chest. "You said something about your side. You were injured in battle, weren't you?"

The earl's right hand unconsciously rubbed up and down Jennie's bare arm as he returned into his memories. "We were caught unawares. We were to leave for home in less than a week and thought we had seen the last of battle. I don't know where the enemy came from; we had thought we were in a safe place behind the lines. I took a piece of exploding shell in my side, and Denny . . . and Denny . . ."

Jennie touched her fingers to his lips. "Shhh. Don't talk about it. Don't think about it."

Kit covered her hand with his own and placed a slow kiss on her palm before laying her hand on his chest. "I have to talk about it. I never have—not to anyone. Maybe if I tell someone, these damned dreams will stop and you and Leon can get some sleep," he quipped, vainly trying to inject some humor into the tense atmosphere.

"I must have been knocked unconscious for a while," he pursued doggedly after a short pause when he seemed to retreat inside himself, talking as if he were reciting a lesson by rote. "When I woke up, the first thing I noticed was the pain in my side. And then the blood—there was blood all over me. Everywhere men and horses were screaming, and smoke stung my eyes. I looked around for Denny, but I couldn't find him. I crawled on my hands and knees in the dirt, looking for him, calling for him . . ."

"Oh, Kit, please stop—"

"No!" he nearly shouted, staring at the ceiling. "I have to say it. I dragged myself over to where Denny's mount lay, a bloody hole in his belly, and that's when I saw him. When . . . when they found me I was still trying to put Denny back together." He turned toward Jennie, his eyes burning fiercely as he tried to explain. "I tried, kitten, I really tried. But . . . but the pieces . . . the pieces didn't fit."

Jennie could stand no more. "Stop it! Please, Kit, stop it!" she pleaded, sobbing as she hid her face in his neck while one bunched fist beat ineffectually against his chest. Kit grabbed at her hand and tried to calm her, suddenly cast into the role of comforter, but his words had taken the innocent child named Jennie and rudely catapulted her into the real world, where sometimes the handsome knights did not prevail.

He rose up, pushing Jennie onto her back and catching her flailing arms above her head. "Jennie . . . kitten . . . hush, sweetheart. I'm sorry," he crooned as her hurt whimpers slowly subsided.

Did he know that her tears were for him? For him, and for Denny, and for all the soldiers who were still dying in that awful, awful war? "No, Kit," she whispered huskily, "don't be sorry. I didn't mean to cry. It's just that it's all so awful . . . so cruel—"

He looked down into her tear-bright eyes and confused, defeated expression, and his heart swelled with fierce, unfamiliar feelings for this caring, compassionate girl who cried for him. "Jennie ... kitten ... I ... *oh, God,*" he groaned passionately as his mouth came down over hers.

Chapter Six

Nothing could be this comfortable, this delightfully warm and soft. Jennie couldn't suppress a small sigh as she snuggled more deeply into the cocoon of creature comfort provided by Kit's embrace—although her sleep-befogged mind had yet to identify it as such. She was too intent on indulging herself in a few more moments of blissful sensuality, allowing the demands of her pleasure-seeking body to keep her mind uninformed as to its actual source. But nothing, not even such innocent bliss, can last forever, and at long last, Jennie began to surface from her slumber.

Stretching out one small hand, she encountered a smooth expanse of warm flesh that she instantly recognized as Kit's bare left shoulder. Her entire body stiffened and her huge green eyes opened wide as the events of the previous night came rushing into her consciousness willy-nilly. "Oh, Lord!" she whispered almost under her breath. "What have I done?"

Slowly, praying all the while, she tilted her head back until she could see her husband's face. Her prayers were answered—he was still sound asleep. If her luck only held until she managed to disentangle herself from his slack hold, she could escape to her own chamber, hide her traitorous body beneath her covers, and try to pretend nothing had happened. Please, she silently entreated any kind spirits who might have been listening, just let me get away from here without waking him.

Slowly, and with incredible stealth, she backed her body toward the side of the large bed and angled one foot toward the floor, which was maddeningly far away. Ducking her head, she slipped Kit's right arm into position across his own chest and allowed her arms to trail behind her as her other foot hit the floor and she slid her body over the edge of the mattress. Another inch or two and she would be completely free of the bed. She held her breath as she slid closer and closer to the floor, releasing it in a long sigh only as her knees made contact with the rug. She'd made it! Now all she had to do was find her nightgown, wherever the dratted thing was, and steal across the room to the adjoining door. She gave a slight shiver—it was rather cold on the floor—and adjusted her plan. She could send Goldie to retrieve the nightgown later, even if it meant she'd have to listen to the maid's sly jokes. She could not dare remaining in Kit's chamber much longer, or else Leon might arrive to wake his master only to catch a glimpse of one hastily departing naked countess. Weighing her options in the twinkling of an eye, she chose Goldie as the lesser of two evils.

Jennie swiveled on the balls of her feet and prepared to creep across the wide expanse of carpeting that lay between her and safety, and had in fact begun to take a small step when her head was enveloped in a cloud of sheer white silk. Her nightgown! Where had that come from?

"Good morning, wife," came a calm male voice.

"Going somewhere? Surely you'll wish your night-gown?"

Jennie looked over her shoulder and upward to see Kit's leering face looking down at her from the edge of the mattress. That he was actually there looking down at her was bad enough, but to know that she could see him almost as clear as day *through* the nightgown still covering her head was enough to send her into an immediate attack of hysterics.

"Close your eyes, you lecher!" she yelped in a most unloverlike way. While Kit obligingly hid his eyes (though not his wide smile) behind his hand, Jennie struggled with the cursed nightgown, nearly ripping it as she fought her way through its folds to find the neck and arm openings hidden there.

"All right, you beast, you may open your eyes now," she said as she laid her hand on the door-knob in anticipation of showing him nothing more than her rapidly departing skirts.

"Hey, kitten, wait a moment!" Kit called after her as she disappeared on the other side of the closed door. "You haven't even given me my morning kiss. And after last night, too," he ended on an exaggerated sigh of longing.

Jennie's head reappeared through the partially opened door just long enough for her to say a highly colorful, definitely improper word and disappear again, leaving Kit to howl in delight at her display of temper.

Once safe in her own room and under the covers just as she had planned, Jennie bit down hard on the soft cushion of her thumb as she struggled with the memories that now crowded into her mind. Had she really allowed him to . . . encouraged him to . . . aided him in his desire

to—oh, Lord above, she *had*! How could she ever
hold her head up in his presence after her shame-
less behavior?

But it had seemed so right, felt so right at the
time. She had been listening to his nightmare,
comforting him. When had everything changed?
How had she reverted from the comforter to the
comforted, and when did the comforting turn into
something deeper, something infinitely stronger
than the mere wish to give each other ease?
Somehow, without her knowledge, compassion had
become passion, and that passion had led to . . .

Well, her common sense intruded, never mind
now just where it had led. She poked her head
out from under the covers to check the time on
the mantel clock, planning to calculate how soon
Goldie would be barging in with her morning
chocolate, and came nose to nose with a smirking
Lord Bourne.

"Up for air, are you?" he questioned cheekily
before vaulting casually onto the mattress to lie
at his ease on his side, one hand propping up his
head as he gazed up at Jennie just as if he weren't
the most obnoxious, insufferable beast in creation. "You dashed off before I could claim a kiss
from my dear bride. *Tsk, tsk,* how naughty you
are, puss," he said with a sad shake of his dark
head. Reaching up, he snaked a hand around the
back of her head, pulling her down to within an
inch of his smiling mouth. "Pucker up now, sweetings, and give your husband his due."

"I'll give you a punch in the chops," Jennie
retorted, wrenching her head from his grasp.

Kit allowed his head to plop down onto the
pillow. "Oh, woe is me," he mourned in mock
dejection, "the chit spurns me. And after all we

were to each other. I believe I am cut to the quick."

How dare he! Jennie thought, incensed. He has taken what had been a beautiful—although, perhaps, in the clear light of hindsight, unfortunate—interlude and turned it into an object of fun. Does he spare my blushes, even a little? He does not. Has he so much as the slightest consideration of my finer feelings? He has not. Does he show the least bit of shame for having taken such elaborate liberties with my person? Far from it. So what does he do? He crashes in here and tries to make a May game out of me, that's what he does! Her fury getting the better of her, Jennie grabbed hold of her pillow and swung it square at Kit's head.

"Hey, what's all that about?" the laughing earl protested, grabbing the fluffy pillow and throwing it to the floor, where his prone body, having been the recipient of Jennie's none too gentle shove, soon joined it.

"Get out of my chamber!" she ordered, hanging over the edge of the bed, the better to shout at him—a tactical mistake that soon had her body joining his on the rug. "At the risk of understatement, Lord Bourne," she intoned crushingly, once she had caught the breath her ignominious fall had knocked out of her, "I *loathe* you!"

It had taken him a while—quite a good while, actually—but at last Kit realized that Jennie wasn't just putting up a token show of anger. She really meant it—she hated the sight of him. How strange, thought the intelligent, but still rather young Earl of Bourne—so perhaps his confusion was excusable. How very strange. My recollections of last night are far from unpleasant. Surely she couldn't be finding fault with my performance.

After all, I know she has no way of comparing me to another, and even in the heat of the moment I can tell the difference between a cry of distress and a cry of passion. And that was passion last night, sure as check, he assured himself in self-defense.

Perhaps if Kit had been older, had a few more years of exposure to the gentler sex under his belt, he would have realized that Jennie was too shy, too inexperienced, to find any pleasure in verbally rehashing the events of the previous evening. An older man might have handled the "morning after" with a good deal more finesse than had Kit. But Kit was not older or more experienced. And he had bungled his role of loving husband—bungled it badly—and now he would have to pay the piper.

Or would he? As he fought to control Jennie's flailing limbs without injuring her, Kit slowly began to get angry. What was the chit carrying on about, anyway? he reasoned with typical male logic. It wasn't as if *he* had entered *her* chamber in the middle of the night dressed in next to nothing and hopped into *her* bed, was it? No! And was it he who had cradled her in his arms and shed sweet tears for her? Again, no! And if he reacted in the same way any red-blooded male animal would react when put into the same circumstances, he'd be damned if he'd spend the rest of his life wearing sackcloth and ashes like some dreadful sinner. If there was blame to be placed in this whole business, then let it rest on the head that deserved it—Jennie's!

"Here now!" he exclaimed, grabbing Jennie by the shoulders and pressing her back against the carpet. "Fun's fun and all that, kitten, but me-

thinks thou dost protest too much, After all, it
was you who seduced me, y'know."

"*Me*! Seduce *you*!" Jennie screeched in disbelief, her body shocked into rigidity. "Well, if that
isn't above all things stupid. You ruin me, and
then you have the gall—the absolute gall—to
blame me for my own ruination?"

"Ruination, is it?" Kit retorted acidly. "That's
a bit strong, don't you think, Jennie? After all,
we are married. Besides," he ended, softening a
little as his ego surfaced, "it wasn't all that bad,
was it?"

"Oh!" Jennie exploded, rising to her feet to
brush her tangled gold locks out of her eyes.
"The conceit of the man!" Dramatically pointing
toward the door, she pronounced regally, "Get
out, my lord, or I shall tell you just how *bad*
things could really become if I put my mind to it,
sirrah!"

Kit took in Jennie's thunderous expression, mentally complimenting the accuracy of his memory
when it was applied to his recollections of the
sweet curves hardly concealed by her thin nightgown, and slowly got to his feet. "All right, puss,
I'll leave. But try as you might, my dear, last
night did happen, and it happened because you
came into my chamber, not through any fault of
my own."

"I only entered your chamber because of your
nightmare," Jennie protested weakly, hating to
see any logic in Kit's statement.

"Perhaps. And, if I have not mentioned it before, I do now thank you, kitten," he said, sobering for a moment. "But you stayed to comfort me
after I awoke, didn't you?" he pointed out, driving his point home with a vengeance. "How dare

you stand there and tell me I'm a cad just because I took what was offered me!"

"Well," Jennie returned, determined to brazen it out, "how dare you be angry with *me* for having the *audacity* to be angry with *you!*"

That piece of feminine reasoning was beyond Kit, and he belatedly saw the wisdom in returning to his own chamber before things became so muddled that Jennie ran home to her father in a pet. He had enough on his plate without that! Left alone, Jennie might eventually see their unplanned lovemaking in a more charitable light, and him along with it. Not that he would pine away to nothingness if she never shared his bed again, but damn it all anyway, he had rather enjoyed her company, even if she hadn't been the bride of his choice.

Left alone once more, Jennie launched her body onto the bed and indulged herself in a cleansing bout of tears which settled absolutely nothing, but at least kept Goldie and Bundy from asking too many questions.

His master was in a fine temper this morning, Leon mused placidly as he deftly caught the spoiled cravat that went winging past his shoulder and handed his lordship a fresh one. That it had something to do with the young countess Leon was certain, but since Renfrew, that old stickler for propriety, had pulled him away from the door last night, Leon was left to ponder whether or not the rumpled state of the bed had anything to do with it. It was unusual for his old major to keep anything from him, Leon having served as his batman in Spain, but the servant instinctively knew that he was not soon to become privy to this latest secret.

His toilette having suffered sadly for his haste, Kit left his valet to straighten the mess his dressing room had become and slammed out of his chamber, intent on quitting the mansion without breakfast and heading for the nearest club that saw nothing wrong with a purely liquid breakfast. Grabbing the stair rail, Kit swung himself onto the stairs and pelted toward the foyer, only to be stopped in his tracks by a reedy cockney voice exclaiming: "Coo, Del, wouldya clap yer glims on the fine gentry mort! Puss like a thundercloud 'e's got. 'ang me fer a bachelor's sprig iffen it ain't the earl 'imself."

The object of this speech inclined his head and took in the sight of three banty-legged creatures dressed in Wilde livery standing at some semblance of attention near the wide front door. He knew what they were supposed to be, they were supposed to be footmen, but they looked for all the world to be escapees from Newgate—low toby men who made their living by picking pockets and breaking into people's houses. *Another example of my wife's discerning judgment of character*, he decided angrily. *But these three cutpurses make Goliath and Tiny look like the cream of the crop!* Forcing his feet to carry him closer, he stopped on the bottom step and introduced himself.

"See, Del, Oi told ya it were 'im," the first footman said to the man standing closest to him before turning to his employer. "Mornin', guv'nor," he chirped, tugging at his nonexistent forelock with one grubby hand. "Oi be Bob, m'self, an' this 'ere be Del an' 'is little brother, Ben. We's yer new footmen, like."

It had been a rough morning so far for the earl and he was not in any mood for this. What he was in the mood for was yelling, which he pro-

ceeded to do. "The bloody hell you are! You'll
damn well be out of my house before I get home,"
he railed at them as Bob hastened to open the
front door. "And *without* the family silver, or I'll
bloody well turn you over to the constable!" he
added, sticking his head back in the door before
taking himself off down the steps and bounding
up behind his pair of blacks and giving them the
office to start.

"D'ya really think 'e'll set the bus-napper on
us?" Del asked Bob in a quavering voice.

"He most assuredly will *not*!" replied a feminine voice, and the three small men turned to see
Miss Ernestine Bundy descending the staircase,
twin flags of color lighting her otherwise sallow
face. "Not that I approve of you—er—*gentlemen*
for one moment, you understand. If it were up to
me I'd have you all out of here before your feet
even knew they were moving. But it was Miss
Jane—I mean, Lady Bourne—who had the hiring
of you, and it is she and only she who can have
the firing of you. It is only fitting—as his lordship, being away in the wilds of Spain for these
past years, must surely have forgotten. Such a
breach of etiquette," she sighed, shaking her head
at the earl's indiscretion. "Lord knows I'll have
my hands full trying to keep this household within
the bounds of courtesy and propriety."

"Whew, boys, there's a 'ell of a goer, iffen ever
Oi clapped my peepers on a finer piece!" Bob
pronounced, awestruck, as he watched Miss Bundy's departing back disappearing into the morning room. "Kinda puts me in mind of mine aunt."

"Yer not sayin' that rum blowen is anythin'
like that bawd in Tothill who calls herself an
abbess—'er wit that covey of barber chairs and
bats she calls 'er girls?"

Ben cuffed Del's ear in reprimand—for how dare he call Miss Bundy a whore? Miss Bundy was a fine lady, that's what she was; and if she were an abbess, he'd bet his eye and Betty Martin she'd have a better stable than one filled with bawds common enough to be called bats or barber chairs! To the uneducated, like Renfrew, who was listening to this interchange with great interest from the other side of the drawing-room door, a barber chair was a whore so common she allowed a whole parish to sit in her to be trimmed, and a bat—why, that unfortunate creature was no more than an ugly whore who could only get a customer after dark, when no one could see her face. In consideration, it might be seen as a good thing that Renfrew's education was lacking in this area, for not even Miss Bundy would prevail if Renfrew got on his high horse and decided Ben, Del, and Bob must go.

Del, holding his injured ear and sniveling into his sleeve, apologized to Ben, obviously the leader of the small gang, and peace once more reigned in the foyer. The three then took up positions on the long bench and rubbed their hands in eager anticipation of the vails the Bourne guests would offer them when they visited, and the revenge they would wreak on any so silly as to try to slip them a bum copper.

Kit was chirping merry by noon. By three he was half seas over, and by five of the clock he was quite in his altitudes, which was how Ozzy Norwood found him when he sauntered into the club.

"Kit, old fellow, how goes it?" Mr. Norwood inquired genially, sitting himself down in the chair next to his friend. "Dashed early in the day to be so deep in your cups, isn't it? What's to do? Surely it can't be your lovely wife who has you diving into the bottom of a bottle—and more than one, by the looks of it. What's forward? Bad news from the Peninsula?"

Kit looked up at his friend from beneath his furrowed eyebrows. "Ozzy," he remarked, spearing the man with his eyes, "you've known me almost all my life. Can you recall any great sin, any terrible crime, I may have committed in that time that I should be so cruelly persecuted now?"

"Persecuted, Kit?" Ozzy repeated, clearly at sea. "Nonsense, man. You're an earl, you're neck deep in money and estates, and your wife is the prettiest thing I've seen in three Seasons. You're *blessed*, man, not persecuted."

"She hired a black giant named Tiny and a dwarf who calls himself Goliath to man my stables. I've got three low-life felons guarding my front door and a pregnant tweeny sniffling and sniveling her way up and down the hallways, and heaven only knows what other surprises await me in the remainder of the staff. And if that's not bad enough, I now have a wife who seduces me and then says it's *my fault*! What do you call that, Ozzy, rolling in the lap of happiness and pure bliss?"

While Kit's first comments did no more than extract a small, bemused smile from his friend, his last statement had Ozzy eagerly pulling his chair closer, his tongue nearly hanging out as he silently urged his friend to continue his monologue.

Lord Bourne leaned back in his chair, cradling his glass between his fingers. "Ah, I have got your attention, have I, Ozzy? Were I not so well and truly corned, I should die before admitting it, but Jennie has me as you see me, totally

beyond thought of my own dignity. I shouldn't be
telling you this," he went on, leaning confidingly
in his friend's direction, "but I find myself in
quite a quandary. It seems I had a bit of a nightmare last night—something I won't go into now—
and my dear virgin bride, overhearing my calls
of terror, came into my chamber to comfort me.
Came into my bed, actually," he added as a sort
of afterthought. "Anyway," he pressed on, pulling a face as he tried to concentrate his mind on
what he was saying, "I woke up to the sight of
my half-naked wife with her arms around me.
Well, one thing led to another, so to speak, and
suddenly we . . . er, never mind."

"Are you quite sure?" Ozzy inquired shakily,
trying not to sound as eager as he felt. "Really,
old man, I'm more than willing to listen to whatever you have to say. Go ahead, Kit, it's me, your
old schoolboy chum—pour your heart out!"

Kit was drunk, but he wasn't totally beyond
rational thought. Smiling a secret smile, he said
shrewdly, "Use your imagination, Ozzy, if you
cannot rely on your own experience. Perhaps you
may have read a book—I do believe I once recall
your saying you have read a book—that will explain the interlude that followed."

"Spoilsport," Ozzy commented gloomily, pushing out his full lower lip in a disappointed pout.

Kit laughed, although his humor did not last
long. "Down, Ozzy, you're making a spectacle of
yourself, salivating like that. I don't know why I
am talking about this with you anyway, seeing
as how you're not married and are unacquainted
with the vagaries of the female mind."

"I am not. I have three sisters, you know,"
Ozzy pointed out mulishly. "You're the one lack-

ing in experience—I've years of trying to cope
with females."

"And have you learned anything?" Kit was so
desperate as to ask.

Ozzy nodded his head vigorously. "I learned
not to try to understand 'em. They're kind of like
good whiskey—you don't try to analyze how it
came to be, you just enjoy it."

"Yes, well, that may work well enough for you,
but then you're not sitting here getting pie-eyed
trying to figure out how you came to be the
guilty party just because you made love to your
own wife—and mighty good lovemaking it was, if
memory serves. Well, I'll tell you this," Kit said
earnestly, his liquid libations making him a little bit pot-valiant, "it'll be a cold day in hell
before I'll let that silly chit dictate to me! I am
master in my own house, and I'll not have some
wet-behind-the-ears child cast me in the role of
villain. In fact," he said, rising rather unsteadily
from his chair, "I think I'll go home now and tell
her so. And I'll jolly well toss her three footmen
onto the flagway, just for good measure!"

"Good evening, gentlemen," came a silky voice
from behind Kit. "Ozzy, mind if I join you? It
seems my friends are late."

Ozzy got to his feet and extended his hand to
the modishly attired gentleman who had spoken.
"Dean, how good to see you. Where have you
been? It's been an age."

Kit subsided into his chair, somewhat awestruck
by the sight of the man Ozzy introduced as Dean
Ives, a tallish, thin young sprig of fashion whose
top-of-the-trees appearance would have made Leon
weep with ecstasy. Mentally comparing the dashing Mr. Ives with the rather short, chubby Mr.
Norwood, Kit could find little that would make

anyone believe these two had a single thing in common. Yet, Kit noticed as the two fell into conversation, it seemed as if they were almost bosom chums—or had been until Kit returned to town and began monopolizing so much of Ozzy's time.

Why this friendship should bother Kit he had no idea, except for the rather selfish one that had him realizing that he had always quite enjoyed the near hero worship with which he had always been treated by Ozzy. Perhaps that is why he regarded Dean Ives in a rather cynical light, listening to the man's conversation for no more than a few minutes before deciding him to be an overly ambitious, vainglory sort of fellow, and a moody chap into the bargain. I'll bet he used to tie cats to trees and light their tails, he thought nastily, curling his lip. He couldn't suppose anyone more totally opposite to the mild-mannered, foot-in-mouth Ozzy if he tried.

It may have been this uneasiness, or this selfishness, that changed Kit's mind and had him accompanying Ozzy and Dean on a round of drinking and gambling rather than returning home to have it out with his wife. Kit didn't know.

He did know, even as tipsy as he was, that it was definitely the lesser of two evils.

Chapter Seven

Two days had passed since "it," as Jennie tended to think of the incident, had happened—two days during which she had spent her time variously devising ways to avoid her husband and wishing he would present himself so they could have it out once and for all.

At eleven of the clock on the morning of the second day, Renfrew entered the drawing room and presented his mistress with a heavily embossed card. "Miss Lucille Gladwin to see you, my lady," he said, making her perusal of the calling card an unnecessary exercise. "Shall I tell her you are not at home?"

"Lucille Gladwin?" Jennie pondered aloud, tapping the edge of the card against her teeth. "Lucy Gladwin!" she exclaimed at last, her memory having been sufficiently nudged so that she recalled a distant cousin named Lucy—a rather rough-and-tumble tomboy, if her recollections were correct. "Oh, dear, can it really be she? Send her in at once, Renfrew. She's m'cousin, you know, and I shouldn't like to think we've kept her waiting."

Jennie rose and moved toward the door, her hands held out in front of her, and Lucy hastened into her cousin's embrace. "Thank goodness, Jane," the bubbly brunette vision in stylish pink-and-green sprigged muslin exclaimed. "For a moment

there I thought you had forgotten me, not that
you'd ever be so shabby as to forget the cousin
who nearly drowned you in the lake. But, I tell
you sincerely, it gave me quite a turn to be standing out there in the foyer with those footmen of
yours. I had the uneasy feeling they were toting
up the price of every stitch on me and planning
their resale in Petticoat Lane."

"Not really, Lucy," Jennie laughed, leading her
cousin to the settee, "but I would advise you to
give them generous vails on the way out if you
ever plan to set foot in Berkeley Square again."

"Jane, dear, I can't believe it! Look at you,
you're all grown up!" Lucy exclaimed, bouncing
up and down on the settee like a child who'd just
been offered a treat. "I'm prodigiously sorry I
haven't been to see you sooner, but Papa had
banished me to the hinterlands for some folly or
other I committed—I disremember right now
which one it was—and I only just saw the wedding announcement in the *Gazette* when I returned to town and caught up on my reading of
the back editions. One must always strive to stay
au courant with the gossip, you know. So tell me,
however did you snare an earl? I'm hanging out
for one myself, you understand, and making a
dashed mishmash of it so far, so you see my
interest is truly self-serving."

Jennie made a face. "Actually, it was quite
easy, Lucy. I just got caught in an animal trap,
impulsively impersonated a village lass, was then
punished for my sins by means of the earl's hap-
hazard attempt at seduction, and *ta-da*—I'm a
countess! It was really prodigiously simple."

"He *compromised* you!" Lucy chortled happily,
clapping her hands in glee. "Oh, how delightfully
romantic. And now, of course, the two of you are

madly in love and about to live happily ever
after. Jane, you always were the lucky one."

"And you were always twice the dreamer I
was," Jennie returned, forcing a laugh.

Lucy was not so overcome with her visions of
true love not to notice the unhappiness in her
cousin's eyes. "Jennie," she inquired concernedly,
using her childhood pet name for her younger
relative, "I know Christopher Wilde has something of a reputation as a womanizer, but I have
it on the best authority that he has not so much
as a single dasher in keeping since his return
from the war. Oh, dear," she went on, seeing
Jennie's frozen expression, "I fear I have shocked
you."

"Not really, Lucy," Jennie assured her. "Association with Kit has taken me a long way from
the schoolgirl miss you remember. I am a woman
now, a wife—more's the pity."

Lucy sensed a juicy story somewhere and leaned
forward, intent on prying every single detail out
of her cousin, which was not a difficult thing to
do considering Jennie's unhappiness and her natural reluctance to confide in Miss Bundy.

Within a very few minutes Lucy, wearing a
sympathetic expression worthy of the most compassionate father confessor, had the whole of it,
and her indignation knew no bounds. "That cad,"
she pronounced severely. "That unmitigated cad!
Well, I can see I have arrived on the scene none
too soon. How dare Kit—I shall call the monster
Kit, since you do—incarcerate you in this great
mausoleum whilst he gads about town like some
carefree bachelor out on a spree? And then to *use*
you like some sort of unpaid mistress—why, it is
the outside of enough, I vow it is. Shabby, absolutely shabby!"

Jennie, although embarrassed at having bared her innermost secrets to Lucy, cousin or not, was intrigued. Here, she thought, was a true woman of the world—a woman who had three London Seasons beneath her belt. Surely Lucy would know just what to do, just how she should go on. If she were to put herself in Lucy's hands—as her cousin had already so kindly suggested—Kit would never know what hit him!

" 'ere ya go, dearie, tea an' cakes, jus' like that old buzzard Renfrew said fer us ta bring ya. Sit up now, dearies, and 'ave at it." Lucy raised her head at this interruption and her mouth dropped open in amazement at the sight of two mirror-image dyed-blond women of indeterminate years, their faces made up like the lowest of painted harridans and their full figures tightly contained in the uniforms of parlor maids. They looked, she thought dizzily, like characters from one of Sheridan's lesser plays—a farce, no doubt.

Jennie looked up at the newcomers, smiled kindly at their appearance in the uniforms she had ordered made for them, and bade them put their burden on the table. "Thank you, Tizzie. You too, Lizzie, although I must remind you once again, it is not necessary for you to follow along in Tizzie's footsteps constantly. You must learn to operate independently of your sister sooner or later. Not that I'm reprimanding you," she added hastily as Lizzie seemed about to burst into tears.

The maids dropped elegant curtsies worthy of a matched set of duchesses and departed, watched all the way by the greatly intrigued Lucy, who felt she had somehow been catapulted onto the stage at Drury Lane. "I give up, cousin," she said when at last she could find her voice, "Who or what were they? If I had been drinking, which I must point out is something I never do since that sad incident at Vauxhall last year, I would vow I was seeing double."

Jennie laughed, Lucy's bewildered expression banishing the last of her doldrums. "Those were my new housemaids. I have hired quite a bit of staff since my arrival in London. Tizzie and Lizzie are 'resting'—as actresses say when they are out of work. Of course, since they have been resting for the past eighteen months or more, I do believe they should revise that and say merely that they have chosen to retire. Not that they had not tried to find employment on the stage; but there is little call for identical twins nowadays—especially female twins 'on the windy side of forty,' as Tizzie explains it. The poor dears were desperate, you know. I had no other option but to employ them. After all, only a heartless creature could cast two such helpless lambs out into the street."

Lucy dissolved in giggles as her memory was jogged by Jennie's story. "Oh, Jennie, how this takes me back! Do you recall the summer you were ten and I was sent—much against my wishes, you know, since I was all of fourteen—to bear you company while our fathers went gadding off somewhere in the wilds to hunt some poor defenseless animals? I'll never forget Simpkins, the groom you employed in your papa's absence. He was wanted for murder or something, wasn't he?"

"He was not!" Jennie protested vehemently. "Well," she temporized, "I guess he was, at least a little bit, wasn't he? But it was all a misunderstanding, you know. Anyone of any sense could see Simpkins wouldn't harm a fly. And I was proved correct in the end, if you'll recall, and Simpkins was exonerated from all charges. He's still on the estate, you know," she added complacently, "although Papa refused to keep him on as groom after he fed Papa's favorite stallion half his pork pie one afternoon when he was too fatigued to fork out a new load of hay. Simpkins is now in sole charge of Papa's guns and fowling pieces—it seems he has an uncanny knack for firearms."

"I wonder why," Lucy pondered, tongue in cheek.

Wiping her hand daintily on a napkin after disposing of two of the sugar cakes served on the tray, Jennie changed the subject and began pumping Lucy on the various social doings currently on the agenda in town, and her cousin was soon prattling nineteen to the dozen about the many routs, balls, and parties the two of them could attend just as soon as she put it about that the new Countess of Bourne was ready to enter Society. "Lady Sefton's card party is tonight, and my invitation extends to include a second person. It will be prodigiously boring, but Sefton is such good *ton*, you know. What say we launch you this very evening? After all, if you wait for that disagreeable husband of yours to take you about, all your new gowns will be sadly out of date."

Talk of gowns soon led the two women upstairs for a critical perusal of the countess's new wardrobe. Goldie, sitting in a corner where she was repairing a rent in one of Jennie's underslips with large stitches and unmatched thread, was quietly amazed at the thoroughness with which Miss Gladwin inspected and disposed of first one outfit and then another, at last deciding on a demure yet stylish white silk frock decorated with blue stitching at the neckline and hem.

Goldie was then called front and center and given detailed instructions on the proper way of dressing her mistress's hair—casually upswept in the Grecian manner, with only a few seemingly haphazardly cascading curls dangling at her nape, a charge which left Goldie speechless, as it was the only style she knew. The maid curtsied and fled the room, part of her unbelieving of her good luck, and the rest of her shaking with the fear that one day Miss Gladwin would demand another hairstyle entirely.

Miss Bundy, entering from the hallway just as Goldie sped by, head down and muttering something that sounded much like "woe is me," took in the situation at a glance and heaved her shoulders in a heartfelt sigh. "Miss Gladwin, I see it *is* you," she pronounced in much the same tones as one who had just discovered roaches in her larder.

"Ernie! By all that's wonderful, don't tell me you are still above ground. I thought surely Jennie's shenanigans would have put you to bed with a shovel long since." Lucy crossed the room to envelop the stiff person of Miss Bundy in a warm embrace. "Now, now, Ernie," Lucy scolded, stepping back a pace, "don't tell me you still haven't forgiven me for putting that toad in your bed?"

There were times, as Jennie could attest, when Miss Bundy could be the best of all good fellows—although those times were admittedly few and far between—and then again, there were times when the dear lady could be a gargantuan pain in the posterior. Clearly, Jennie could see from the faint rush of scarlet running up the back of her companion's scrawny neck, this was to be one of her less fun-loving days. "Did you have something particular in mind, Bundy, or is this purely a social visit?" Jennie asked as casually as she could, knowing full well Bundy was not above tossing Lucy out on her ear and saying it was on orders from her papa.

"This note just arrived from Boodle's, as you can see by the wax imprint. I would imagine it is from the earl," Miss Bundy informed her, handing the note over unopened—and therefore quite reluctantly.

Jennie ripped open the missive with little regard for the elaborate seal and read the note with ever increasing fury. "The nerve of the man," she said feelingly as she crumpled the missive into a ball and tossed it in the general direction of the fireplace. "He has *ordered* me to reserve two extra places at table tonight for his friends— he who hasn't shared a dinner table with me since our marriage." A martial light came into her eyes as she began pacing back and forth in high dudgeon. "For two pins I'd serve swamp grass on stale toast!" she said wickedly. "That would set him down a peg or two!"

"Pooh," Lucy said breezily. "That's letting the bounder off entirely too easily. Here now," she pronounced firmly, taking in Jennie's woebegone expression, "don't you go turning into a watering pot on me. If it's revenge you want—and I clearly believe you have every right to demand it—I believe I have a sure idea for throwing a bit of a rub in his lordship's way."

Every family had its black sheep, Ernestine Bundy knew, but why the Gladwin girl couldn't have had the good sense to be living in the wild outbacks of Australia or some such place she never would understand. The minute Renfrew had told her the identity of Jennie's visitor, Miss Bundy had felt apprehension flow into her body and become a crushing sensation in her breast. And within minutes of encountering the horrid child the woman's worst imaginings were well on the way to becoming fact. "Now see here, Miss Lucy," she began heatedly, only to be cut off by a languid wave of that young schemer's slim white hand.

"Now, Ernie, don't fly up into the boughs," Lucy warned with a chuckle. "You cannot have lived under the same roof with the newlyweds without sensing something is amiss between them. Jennie cannot allow this situation to go on if she is ever to establish herself as mistress of this household. Now," she said, pacing back and forth as she thought and spoke at the same time, "as I understand it, Kit's impolite order has been issued with no thought to any plans his wife may have made. I see no reason for the master of the house to be denied a dinner at home with his cronies; m'father raised me too well to deny any man on that head. *However,* I likewise see no reason for Jennie to forgo her own plans just because of some last-minute whim of her unthinking husband. Lord Bourne shall have his dinner, sure enough, but Jennie shall also have her night out at Lady Sefton's," she ended triumphantly. "Who said a girl can't have her cake and eat it too!"

"Lady . . . Lady *Sefton?*" Miss Bundy stammered, clearly much impressed. Who would have thought Lucy Gladwin could wrangle such a coveted invitation? Of course, Miss Bundy couldn't deny her baby the chance to move in such exalted circles. Knowing defeat when she tasted it, the companion retired from the field, leaving the two girls to plan and giggle their way through the afternoon.

The Earl of Bourne was dressed all in blue, his

velvet coat a light robin's-egg shade that con-
trasted nicely with his darkest midnight-blue in-
expressibles; the whole set off by a snowy white
lace-trimmed cravat tied in the latest style, and
onyx jewelry of elegant, understated design. Admiring himself in the mirror in his dressing room,
he did not need (though secretly enjoyed) Leon's
flowery praise, believing himself amply armored
for the task at hand—bowling over his recalci-
trant wife with both his charm and his good
looks.

Kit saw this night's tame entertainment as a
foretaste of things to come; a sort of gentle easing into society that would stand Jennie in good
stead for the months of grueling social engagements that loomed ahead of them. Ozzy, he knew,
was the perfect dinner companion for this, their
first entertainment, as the man was as much
renowned for his good *ton* as he was notorious
for his mediocre intelligence. The only fly in the
ointment was in the person of Dean Ives, a man
Kit, even after two days' close acquaintance, just
could not seem to like. But the fellow was a
prime example of a tulip of fashion, one of those
sarcastic, cynical sorts that breezed through the
ton like scraps of yesterday's newspaper blown in
the wind, and Jennie must learn to deal with his
type sooner or later.

One last check of his toilette completed, Kit
bounded down the steps to see if his wife had
preceded him to the drawing room. It wouldn't do
for her to be either overdressed or underdressed.
He could only hope Miss Bundy could be relied
upon to guide her in such matters. But when he
entered the room he realized he had beaten her
downstairs, and he was forced to content himself

with sipping from a glass of wine while he waited for her entrance, which was not long in coming.

She looked wonderful! Kit straightened himself from his lounging position against the mantelpiece and crossed the room hurriedly to place a kiss on the back of her white-kid-encased hand. "You are ravishing tonight, kitten," he drawled smoothly, inwardly delighted when his words brought a warm blush to her cheeks. "You do me proud."

It was now or never, Jennie thought, gently disengaging her hand, which he was still fondling in the most disturbing manner. "Thank you, my lord, for your kind words," she replied in a small voice before moving to stand near the wine decanter in hopes he would take the hint and offer her a drink. Clearing her throat, which suddenly felt strangely dry, she launched into speech before her courage deserted her entirely. "What a shame I shall not be here for dinner, as Montague has planned a veritable feast. Please do try to eat all of it," she added swiftly, her tender heart forcing her to warn him of the French chef's abhorrence of seeing plates returned to his kitchen half full.

Kit did not hear her warning, for he was too intent on the first part of her speech. "What do you mean, you will not be here?" he growled, grabbing her rather fiercely by the elbow. "Did you not receive my note? And where the deuce would you be going anyway? I was not aware you knew a soul in town."

Jennie looked rather pointedly at Kit's restraining fingers before gazing directly into his deep blue eyes (eyes so compelling her resolve nearly melted then and there) and coolly asking him to remove his hand from her person. "I have an invitation to Lady Sefton's card party this evening," she told him with some asperity. "My cousin Lucy Gladwin was kind enough to allow me to share her invitation. You see, husband, I am not destined to molder away in Berkeley Square just because you refuse to do your duty and introduce me to society. I am not entirely without resources of my own."

"Lucy Gladwin!" Kit exploded angrily. "That female disaster? God give me patience!"

Jennie stood up very straight, her chin reaching for the ceiling. "How dare you, sirrah! Lucy is not a disaster but a very dear, sweet person. I will not stand here and allow you to insult her. Have the goodness, sir, to step aside."

"In a pig's eye, I will!" Kit shot back, standing his ground, planting his fists firmly on his hips for good measure. "I am your husband, madam, and I have every right to dictate where you shall go and with whom. Lady Sefton may be unimpeachable, but Lucy Gladwin is next door to a hoyden and no person for you to be seen with either formally or informally. God, madam, I wouldn't be caught dead within twenty feet of that incorrigible minx."

"Then I suggest you retire to your chamber, my lord, for she shall be arriving here at any moment. And if you make a scene, Kit," she warned direly, "I shall lie down on this carpet and throw a tantrum that will have your high and mighty guests dining out on their story of the Earl of Bourne and his mad wife for a month or more. Do I make myself clear, sir?"

"You dare to flout me?" Kit bellowed, clearly losing control of the situation. What imp of perversion had ever made him believe that Jennie was a reasonable, fairly biddable chit? The harridan now staring him down bore all the soft vulnerability of a charging Prussian, and he was at a loss as to how to deal with her.

Luckily, or unluckily, depending on whether or not Renfrew (who was standing outside the door) really desired to know how the argument would have turned out, the sound of the knocker interrupted the sparring pair and they swiftly took up positions at opposite ends of the room to await whatever guest was first to come through the doors.

"Look who we met outside, Kit, old fellow," Ozzy said in greeting as he entered the room, a smiling Lucy Gladwin hanging from his arm and Dean Ives bringing up the rear. "I haven't seen Lucy since that day she raced her curricle against Lord Beazley's in the park. Was that before or after your escapade in the reflecting pool, Lucy? I disremember, seeing as how you're always running some sort of rig."

"Now, Ozzy," Lucy admonished her grinning admirer as she caught sight of Lord Bourne's darkened features, "you mustn't embarrass me by bringing up past indiscretions. Since my sojourn in the country I am a veritable pattern card of respectability. I have to be, else I forfeit my allowance for the next decade, or so says my poor oppressed papa. I beat old Beazley all hollow, by the way," she added with a wink.

Jennie chanced a quick look at her husband and cringed inwardly at the thought he may have been just a teensy bit correct in his assessment of Lucy's behavior. Not that she was about to change her plans at this late date, especially now that he had stated his opposition so adamantly. "Lucy, dearest," she trilled brightly, welcoming her cousin, "you are just in time. If we tarry, Renfrew will be late in calling the gentlemen to dine—a sin of such magnitude I shudder to think how Montague will react. Gentlemen," she went on, curtsying sweetly in the newcomers' direction, "I do not believe we have been formally introduced."

Mr. Norwood, endlessly grateful that Lady Bourne was willing to overlook their first, rather lamentable meeting, hastened to introduce Mr. Ives and himself, as Kit showed every indication of having been stuffed and permanently mounted in front of the mantelpiece. Jennie liked Ozzy even better on this second acquaintance, but there was something about the knowing look in Mr. Ives's handsome face that reminded her of a weasel stalking a mouse. He was, she thought idly, just a little too smooth, a little too handsome for her liking; not like Kit, who had just enough of the raw youth about him to make him seem human.

After the introductions, and knowing full well that Kit wouldn't dare a scene in front of his friends, Jennie made short work out of bustling Lucy out of the house, pausing only to warn the gentlemen to be sure and eat all their peas.

Chapter Eight

Lucy's parting assurance, tossed over her shoulder as Jennie half-dragged her through the foyer, that her maiden Aunt Rachel—just then resting in the Gladwin coach outside—was to serve as their "respectable" chaperon for the evening did little to placate Lord Bourne's raging temper. If left to his own devices, in fact, one could only cringe in fearful anticipation of just what form his anger would take. But he was not given the option of being left alone as he, his weary brain reminded him, had dinner guests. Dinner guests, moreover, whose wide grins showed just a little bit too much enjoyment in their host's predicament.

"Gentlemen," he said with a social smile that failed to hide his chagrin, "I am being a poor host. Allow me to get you each a drink before Renfrew calls us to dinner." So saying, Kit went to the side table and poured three generous drinks, downing his own in one gulp before serving his guests. Get 'em drunk, he thought sagely. Get 'em drunk and they'll never remember in the morning whether a hostess sat at the bottom of the table or not.

When Renfrew summoned the small party to the dining table, Kit pulled the man aside for a moment and whispered his wish that his guests' glasses be topped up whenever they so much as took a sip of wine, and Renfrew, having served the Wildes for more years than the present earl had had hot dinners, did not so much as raise an eyebrow at the request.

For the next two hours and more the men feasted on some of the finest victuals served this side of Prinny's table, washing down each course with the best wines to be found in the Bourne cellars. Mr. Ives commented more than once on both the quality and the quantity of both, adding rather tackily his own estimate of the price of each exotic foodstuff and vintage. Indeed, Ozzy was so amused by his friend's assessing remarks that he dared to tease Dean by asking him if he intended to upend the dinner plate and check to see the crest of the manufacturer, a remark that drew a killing look from Mr. Ives and a raised eyebrow from his host.

Although the food, all prepared in the best French style, was everything that Kit could have asked for, the choice of five desserts seemed, to him, to perhaps be overdoing things just a tad. His dinner partners, stuffed chock full of buttered lobster, duckling, a variety of vegetables served in creamy sauces, and other delicacies, were likewise hard pressed to do more than token justice to the impressive array of pastries and cakes that were meant to close their meal. A few bits of cheese and some cracked walnuts were desultorily picked over, but the groaning tray of sweets was returned to the kitchen virtually untouched as the men lit cheroots and leaned back in their chairs to watch Renfrew serve them with generously filled goblets of finest port.

The evening, Kit congratulated himself silently, seemed to be a success, even without Jennie's presence. He'd show the chit just how little she meant to him either way. He admitted that no matter how odd her choice in footmen and maids seemed to be, she had really outdone herself in filling his request for a good French chef. If he hadn't felt so out of charity with her he might have even believed he could be brought to compliment her on her choice. But no, he thought, savoring his small revenge, let her wonder whether or not he was pleased. Keep her dangling, that's the ticket, he decided. If she really wanted to please me she would be sitting opposite me right this very minute instead of gallivanting about town with that inane Gladwin chit.

Drat Jennie anyway! he thought, setting down his goblet with more violence than he had intended, causing his companions to look at him oddly. He had planned this evening as a sort of peace offering—a small introduction to society that, if she conducted herself correctly, would serve as a forerunner to other, larger engagements where he would magnanimously serve as her tutor as she dipped her toes into the stream of high society. She was his wife—certainly there was no way out of the marriage after the events of the other evening—and if she enjoyed herself in London it might make her come around a bit in her feelings for her new husband. Oh, the plan made sense, all right—at least to a man it did—but he had not counted on her finding her own way into society. Instead of being pleased at his efforts on her behalf she had deliberately flouted him, just as if he hadn't had her best interests at heart.

It is amazing how a man can rationalize away his own desires and have them appear as altruistic sacrifices, but then men have since time immemorial assumed they knew what was best for their women and then acted on those assumptions without ever once asking those same women whether or not they wished such a sacrifice. Kit, being no worse or better than any of his fellow male ancestors, was now reacting in a typically male way—if Jennie didn't appreciate what he had done for her, he decided firmly, then he'd be damned for a dolt before he ever did anything nice for her again!

While Kit variously plotted revenge and entertained thoughts of sweetly forgiving Jennie as his fingers made casual inroads on the fastenings of the fetching gown she had worn that evening, Ozzy and Dean, feeling more than a little well to go, idly discussed the possibility of the three of them adjourning to one of the discreet houses on the fringes of Mayfair that specialized in the comforts of lonely men. Ozzy was just about to suggest the White House as one possible destination when there came a loud commotion at the doorway that led back to the kitchen.

"What in blazes?" Kit said irritably, turning in his seat to see what was going on, only to be startled into silence at the sight of the very large, burly man dressed in the all-white uniform of a chef who was at that very moment advancing upon his lordship waving a very menacing-looking meat cleaver. Bob, Ben, and Del, looking about as effectual as minnows trying to swim upstream against a tidal wave, hung from the wild chef's arms and were carried along, their feet nearly a foot above the floor.

"*Sacrebleu!*" the irate Montague bellowed in his deep, highly accented voice. "Show to me the *canaille* who dare fling Montague's tarts back in his face! A work of art, tossed aside like *entrailles*, *bagatelles!* Montague, he shall skewer the *coquin,* of a surety he will!"

"Quick, guv'nor," Ben yelled as Montague turned to shake Del off his arm as a giant flicks away a flea, "make a break for it. Oi've got 'im."

Renfrew slipped from the room, unnoticed in the melee, as Kit, his army training coming to the fore, rose from his chair and delivered a punishing blow directly into Montague's ample midsection, which slowed him down a bit but did not stop him. Ozzy, never much in the way of anything athletic, did his little bit by tossing his goblet full of port at the chef—thinking to cool the man a bit—and then retired from the fray, sliding his pudgy frame under the Sheraton buffet table and his head behind the brass spittoon. Dean Ives, sitting farthest from the scene of the action, merely continued to sip delicately from his goblet and await further developments—which, fortunately for Kit, were not long in coming.

With a crash that set the china and crystal to shaking, the baize door swung back against the wall as Tiny advanced into the room with all the grace of a benevolent gorilla. *"Arrrrgh!"* he growled as his huge, beefy fists encircled Montague's neck and lifted the irate chef a full two feet off the floor, Ben and Bob falling to the carpet like autumn leaves caught in a breeze. Kit dropped his fists and stared, as did everyone else in the room, and it is possible the Frenchman would have choked if Goliath, entering the room in his rapid, skipping gait, hadn't grabbed onto Tiny's pants and climbed up the giant to whisper something in his ear.

Tiny looked at Goliath, who nodded once before sliding back down the mountain to the floor, and Montague, his face a truly lovely shade of

purple, was allowed to live to cook another day.
Bowing in his lordship's direction, Tiny shrugged
his great shoulders shyly, smiled his sweet, stupid grin, and allowed Goliath to lead him from
the room like a tame puppy. His anger effectively choked out of him, Montague—who had
lost more than one job due to his lamentable
temper—lapsed completely into French as he tried
simultaneously to apologize to his master and
hide the deadly cleaver behind his back.

"Now, now, m'lord," Renfrew soothed placatingly
as Kit showed every intention of finishing the job
Tiny had started, "there was no harm done. Lady
Bourne had warned me about Montague's temperament, but somehow I had forgotten about it
and allowed the plate of desserts to go back to
the kitchen without first emptying it. Montague
is a wonderful chef, sir, it's just that he gets a
little touchy about his, er, creations. The rest of
the staff humors him by hiding any leftovers out
of sight—indeed, we have the best-fed staff in all
London town, if I do say so myself, but you know
how it is, every once in a while there's bound to
be a little slip-up. It's just a good job," the man
ended earnestly, "that I remembered about Tiny
in time."

"Yes, Kit," Ozzy put in as he crawled out from
under the buffet. "Your lady *did* warn us to be
sure to eat all our peas. Seems the fault lies with
us—being as how we were put on notice. Now,
now, old fellow," Ozzy went on as Kit showed
some lingering signs of impending explosion,
"think again of that lobster. Would you be so
daft as to give that up just because the man
has a bit of a temper? I call that very poor sporting of you, Kit, in truth I do."

In the end, Montague was allowed to return to

his kitchen—where Ben, Bob, and Del had already effectively removed any remaining bits of evidence by filling their bellies with the riot-causing sweets—and the gentlemen, one still silently fuming, one obviously amused, and one curiously silent, adjourned to the drawing room, where, after a few minutes of rather anticlimactic conversation about such tame doings as the war and other mundane events, the party broke up at the ungodly early hour of eleven.

As Ozzy stepped out the door onto the steps he ventured a parting shot at his friend. "Kit," he said, his lips trembling with suppressed mirth, "I'll say one thing for you—you sure know how to give a fellow a good time. Really, perhaps you ought to give a thought or two to charging admission to your little shows."

"I don't know about that," Kit responded, somehow summoning up a smile. "After all, Ozzy, it's m'wife's menagerie, not mine. You'll have to ask her."

"Oh, her ladyship's a prime right one, I have no fears on that head," Ozzy returned jovially. "Keep this up, Kit, and the Bourne mansion will become *the* place to see and be seen and your lady the premier hostess in the entire *ton*! Give her my regards," Mr. Norwood ended, skipping lightly down the steps to the flagway and saluting his friend before turning to enter his waiting carriage.

"I'll be sure to do that," the earl called after him, his smile becoming a little strained around the edges. Once the carriage had driven off, the smile, which had been frozen on his face like a Gunther ice, melted slowly and reformed itself into a fierce grimace. "Give her my regards, the looby says," he told the night sky before slam ming the heavy front door with a satisfying swipe of his hand. "Of course I will, Ozzy, old fellow—and *then* I'll murder her!

It was just striking two when Jennie came tiptoeing carefully up the stairs to her chamber, her head swimming just slightly from the wine she had imbibed in an effort to overcome the nervousness brought on by her first foray into society. Not that Lucy hadn't been by her side the whole evening, doling out gossip about some of their company while waving gaily to any number of acquaintances who called to her most familiarly as they made their way to tables already set up for tame-stakes gambling.

The card party hadn't been nearly as much fun as Jennie had thought—and certainly not as pleasurable as it should have been, considering she had chanced Kit's wrath in order to attend it. But then *ton* parties, according to Lucy, were for the most part dull as ditchwater. Jennie rather doubted this was true, or else why would Kit attend so many of them? But, she had thought as two of Lady Sefton's footmen carried a happily passed-out earl from the cardroom, perhaps men found amusement more easily come by than women.

No matter what, Jennie was now home again, and she could not help but wonder how Kit's evening had gone. Entering her chamber, her evening slippers dangling from one hand, she was just beginning to make out the shape of her furniture in the near darkness when a movement in the shadows caught her attention.

"Good evening, wife," came Kit's voice, oddly strained. "Much as I hate to upset you, I am I have to tell you that your attempt at assassination failed. Your husband, ma'am, is still very much alive."

"I—I don't understand," Jennie stammered nervously, misliking the strange glitter in her husband's eyes.

Kit advanced on her, his smile making her stockinged toes curl defensively into the carpeting. "Really?" he purred, sliding a hand around Jennie's throat to finger the curls at her nape. "Allow me to refresh your memory. Do the words 'eat all your peas' ring any bells for you, ma'am?"

Jennie's stomach dropped to her knees, and she made a face that looked as if she had just bitten into a rather bitter pickle. "Montague," she breathed softly. "I knew I should have remained at home. Drat Lucy and her fine speeches about putting you in your place."

"Please, kitten," the earl said silkily, his fingers tightening just slightly, "have the decency not to include Miss Gladwin in this particular escapade. She may have been the instigator of your little mutiny tonight, but I know for a fact that it was not she who had the hiring of that maniacal Frenchman. Oh no. Montague bears all the marks of your handiwork." Exerting a bit more pressure, Kit directed Jennie's footsteps toward the bed and pushed her rump down onto it. "Do you have any idea how disconcerting it is to look up from your own dinner table to see death looking you in the eyes? It may serve to put me off my feed for a month. Well?" he asked, staring down into her fear-widened eyes, "Have you nothing to say for yourself?"

It was quiet in the room for some moments while Jennie searched wildly for something to say. At last, her wits deserting her entirely, she gave voice to the only thing that her brain could muster: "Do you not care for green peas, then, my lord?"

Kit dropped into a nearby chair and let his forehead rest on his hands. "God give me patience," he groaned, shaking his weary head. He looked up at Jennie, saw her tear-bright green eyes, and instantly felt as if he had been cruelly mistreating a lost kitten. She was such a baby—such an innocent, trusting baby. She shouldn't yet be allowed out on her own, not with her penchant for picking up strays and bringing them back with her. Unable to vent his spleen by taking vengeance on his wife's nubile body, Kit reached out his hand for the nearest object—which happened to be a rather fine crystal vase—and flung it full force into the cold fireplace. It landed with a satisfying crash, which went a long way toward easing the constriction in the earl's chest, at least for the few moments it took for Goldie and Miss Bundy to burst upon the scene in their nightclothes, anxious to see what was amiss.

Miss Bundy's eyes took in the scene in a glance, and, as she had been informed by Renfrew of the events earlier in the evening, she had no doubt as to what was now taking place. His lordship was merely making a critical statement concerning Jennie's choice of chef.

But Goldie was another matter. In her simple brain the thought formed that her mistress was in dire danger of imminent death—or worse. Racing to Jennie's side, she flung her ample arms wide and pronounced dramatically, "You'll not get ta her lessen it's over me own dead body!"

Miss Bundy, sadly aware that she was standing before his lordship dressed only in her nightgown, but also realizing her intervention was needed, pushed herself into disgusted speech.

"Goldie," she said condemningly, "there are times your ignorance would disgrace a Hottentot. His lordship is not here to do murder; it's just that the vase slipped from his hand as he was making a point in a discussion he was having with Lady Bourne. Now drop the pose of martyr you have struck and remove your scantily clad body from the room posthaste."

Goldie looked down at her coarse white cotton gown and rapidly pulled in her outflung arms to wrap them protectively around her upper body. " 'Pon my soul!" she exclaimed, mortified.

"Upon yours, maybe," Miss Bundy was pushed to say unkindly, "but thank goodness, not upon mine. Now scoot!"

"You want me to leave?" Goldie asked, clearly still of half a mind to stay and protect her mistress.

"What would you suggest as an alternative?" Miss Bundy asked acidly.

From his place in the corner, Lord Bourne was heard to mumble under his breath: "We gather here to lend prayers . . ."

This irreverent aside was too much for Jennie, who laid herself back on her bed and began to howl with relieved laughter. Kit might be an easily lit match, but luckily, he was one whose temper burned brightly for only a moment before common sense and his wonderful love of the ridiculous effectively snuffed the flame.

Within moments of Jennie's delighted chuckling, Miss Bundy had successfully herded the confused Goldie, still vainly trying to cover her "private parts" with her hands (now placed strategically behind her as she scuttled toward the door), and Lord Bourne rose from his seat to lock the door behind them.

"Now, kitten," he began softly once the key

was safely in his breast pocket, "perhaps we can discuss your punishment?"

It was nearing dawn when the earl returned to his own chamber, a man much changed from either the angry one who had waited countless hours for the return of his delinquent wife or the amused one who had waggled his eyebrows in mock menace as he approached his wife's bed, intent only on making her feel a bit of the discomfort he had felt earlier. Now it was a thoughtful earl who paced his chamber, his hands clasped tightly behind his back.

How had things gotten so out of hand? When had teasing turned to something infinitely more intense, and vague thoughts of revenge receded to be replaced by a desire to feel his wife's warm form beneath him as he burned kisses over every inch of her soft body?

Memories of the past hours crowded into his brain, and he could close his eyes and relive every moment, almost as if he had been hovering above the bed looking down at the passionate pair clinging to each other among a tangle of sheets and blankets. Jennie's soft cries, begun in fear but swiftly turning to whimpers of mingled delight and anticipation, echoed disturbingly loud in his ears, and he sank into a chair as his mind recalled the sound of his own voice, soothing, cajoling, reassuring—and, in the end, begging, pleading for blessed release. Never, he told himself passionately, never before in his life had he felt such intensity, such a deep need to possess, to enfold, to cherish. And more—much more.

He could now recapture, with almost physical pain, the rapture he'd felt as Jennie's young head bent to run light kisses the length of the wicked

scar on his side. What had he felt when she had
caressed him so unselfishly? Could that strange
constriction in his throat have been the first stir-
rings of love? "Nonsense!" he nearly shouted into
the early-morning haze. "Utter nonsense! By God,
I don't even *like* the balmy chit. Playing at love,
just as she plays at lady of the manor. Bloody
hell, the idiot picks her companions with all the
discretion and judgment of a child allowed to
choose her own menu—never thinking about a
thing but what tastes good, and giving not a
single thought to what's good for her."

That little speech gave the earl pause. It was
one thing to rationalize away Jennie's predilec-
tion for eccentrics who tugged at her gentle heart,
but it was another to classify himself as one of
her pet projects. Could it be the affection she had
showered on him so freely just a short time ago
had stemmed from some warped idea of hers that
he was in need of her protection and direction,
like Tiny, or Del, or even the volatile Montague?
Did she see him as some sort of misfit, or had her
tender heart been wrung by his tale of Denny
and the wound he had sustained? That would
explain her gentle, ministering attitude, though,
he thought hopefully, it certainly would not explain her passion.

Perhaps the little dreamer had decided that he
was a romantic hero and she believed herself in
love with him. Wouldn't that be a kick in the
head! First he was saddled with the girl as an
unwanted bride, and now he was in danger of
suffering through her first encounter with puppy
love. It was more than any one man could be
expected to bear.

Kit crossed to the connecting door and peeked
in on his sleeping wife, all curled up in a little

ball in the middle of the huge bed and looking for all the world like a sleep-warmed child. His heart did a strange sort of flip-flop in his breast and he was hard pressed not to crawl back beneath the sheets and cradle her golden head on his bare chest. He resisted the impulse, knowing full well he was getting in much too deep for a man whose very last wish in life was to be saddled with an adoring wife.

Returning to his own room once more, he lit a cheroot and went to look out his window onto the square below. She was getting to him, this child bride of his, and he'd be damned if he'd allow her to make further inroads into his self-sufficiency.

Then why, he asked himself on a deep sigh, did his arms feel so damned empty without her?

Jennie held her breath until the door closed, with Kit safely returned once more to his own chamber. He had stood looking down at her for so long she was sure she would give herself away. But just as she felt sure she would have to open her eyes, he had at last turned away. She didn't know why she didn't want him to know she was awake, she only knew she couldn't face him until she had time to think over what had happened between them and come to some sort of conclusion as to just what it all meant.

Had that really been her, Jennie Maitland Wilde, who had behaved with such wild, even wicked, abandon in the wee hours of the night? Could it have been the same Jennie Maitland Wilde who now lay here, shivering in a tight fetal position, striving vainly to pretend to herself that nothing earthshaking had happened? But she could not deny the facts, any more than she could deny the lingering lassitude that had

her twisting slowly between the sheets so that
her suddenly sensitive skin could relive in part
the wonderful, cherished feeling of being held so
tightly in Kit's embrace.

She *was* a wanton—there was no other explanation for it. But how could she help herself,
when Kit was so very handsome, and so very
experienced! That was it! He had seduced her
again! No, her honest self denied as she punched
her pillows and tried once more to find the sanctuary of sleep. He did not seduce me. It was . . . it
was more of a joint seduction, with both parties
equally at fault.

All right, she told herself rationally. It was one
thing to allow oneself to be made love to, but it
was quite another to *initiate* a second round of
lovemaking. And that mad impulse to kiss away
the pain of his scar—why, Bundy would die of
mortification if ever I told her I had been so
forward.

"So why should you be telling Bundy?" she
said aloud, sitting up sharply in the bed. "You
are a married lady now, not some schoolgirl who
must give an accounting of her every move.
Although," she went on, a ghost of a smile lighting her worried features, "it might be interesting
to see Bundy's reaction to a full recitation of last
night's events. For once the roles of tutor and
student would be reversed, I believe." This little
bit of silliness lightened Jennie's somber mood
for a moment, but nothing could keep her mind
overlong from her newest dilemma. It had been
one thing for Jennie to disregard a single "tum-
ble," as Goldie would term it, but it was quite
another to sweep the abandoned lovemaking just
past under the rug and pretend it had not happened.

Besides, she wasn't really sure she wanted to forget. She really believed she might just be doing the unfashionable—falling in love with her own husband. Then another, sobering thought intervened. Obviously Kit did not feel the same, else why would he steal out of her chamber before dawn like some thief? Couldn't he face her in the morning after the things he had whispered into her ear during the night? This put a whole new complexion on the matter, Jennie knew, worrying her bottom lip with her teeth. Now she was more confused than ever, and she mentally tried to hold back the dawn so that she would not have to face her husband over the breakfast table and try to think of something to say other than "Ah, yes, Kit. That—please do *that*!"

Montague outdid himself with the breakfast buffet, the menu offering more varieties of meats and side dishes than the best hotel in London. And, to show his newfound mellow temperament, he did not throw more than three platters against the wall when every offering but the toast was sent back to the kitchen untouched.

Poor Montague. How was he to know that the Bourne morning room, visited separately by the earl and countess in a series of strategic advances and retreats that would have done credit to the wiliest generals, was the last—the very last—place either of the parties would envision as a setting fit to encourage an appetite?

The earl, first down that morning, had done nothing more than order Renfrew to bring him a glass of brown ale before, looking about him like a culprit waiting for the law to clap him on the shoulder, he slipped from the house; and the countess, who had tiptoed to and from the morning-room door three times before deciding it was safe to enter, had done no more than nibble at a crust of toast before, even bearing in mind the great stress her actions were placing on Montague, she too ignobly retired from the field.

As this strange dance of advance and retreat, this playing of stay-least-in-sight, was to go on for over a week, it was no wonder that Bob, Ben, and Del were soon applying to Charity—the poor, dear thing—to let out their uniforms at the waist. After all, as Bob said repeatedly as he downed yet another light French pastry, *somebody* had to keep the balmy froggie from murdering them all in their beds!

Chapter Nine

"This building is relatively new, you know," Lucy told Jennie as the other girl sat in the Gladwin private box and stared about her openmouthed. "Covent Garden burned down in 1808, I believe it was, and all this had to be rebuilt."

"It's beautiful . . . simply beautiful!" Jennie told her cousin in awestruck tones. "It must have cost a fortune."

Lucy laughed, partly at Jennie's naive gawking and partly at her naive observation. "Indeed it did, cousin. So much so, in fact, that the owners tried to raise the prices to pay for it. Did you never hear of the O.P. riots?"

"O.P. riots?" Jennie repeated questioningly. "No, I can't say as I have. Were they very bad?"

"That, dear coz, depends on whether you were one of the owners or one of the paying public. For the owners, I daresay it was a disaster. As for the public, I do believe it was a bit of a lark. The gentlemen in the pits as well as those in the galleries spent night after night throwing oranges at the stage, rattling rattles, blowing horns, shouting and stamping their feet—even singing songs specially written for the occasion. All to get a rollback to the *Old Prices*. It really did dampen the actors' enthusiasm for appearing on stage."

"Oh my," Jennie observed, feeling much in sympathy with the poor actors. "Do you really think that was fair?"

"Fair or not, it must have been great fun. I only wish I had been 'out' in time to participate. Why, I can remember Papa going off to the theater wearing his special O.P. hat on his head and his custom-made O.P. medal on his breast. The ladies, as I recall, had fans, handkerchiefs, oh, all sorts of things, embroidered with the letters O.P., and there was barely a building in all London that did not have those initials scribbled on its walls. Papa said it was the best of good fun—what with the whole of the audience spending every night at the theater, dancing, singing, and jumping back and forth on the benches. The prices," Lucy ended happily, "were quite naturally rolled back. After all, no one can stand for long against the might of a combined assault of good, honest Englishmen."

"Oh, Lucy, you should have been born a man," Jennie said, taking in the brightness of her cousin's expression.

But the smile slowly faded from Lucy's face as she caught sight of a couple in a box across the way, "Not really, coz," she said solemnly. "Don't make it too obvious, but take a look across the way at the box three to the left of the Royal Enclosure." Jennie made a fuss of adjusting her fan and peered in the direction Lucy had indicated. "Do you see the fierce-looking old dragon in purple with those absolutely nauseating violet plumes sticking out of her head?" Jennie nodded. "All right," Lucy continued, her voice oddly breathless. "Now look at the man sitting in front of her and to her right. That is Lord Thorpe, the man I am going to marry. *Now* you can see why I am glad not to have been born a boy. Isn't he the most handsome man you've ever seen?"

Jennie trained her eyes on the gentleman in question and could not help but agree that he was a fine-looking specimen of mankind, although she herself had a preference for dark-haired men such as Kit. Besides, Lord Thorpe had the look of the snob about him, just in the way he was casting his eyes about him now in barely concealed boredom. "Who is that girl sitting next to him?" she asked Lucy, thinking that the young female dressed in demure, rather color-robbing white must be the reason for Lord Thorpe's rather pained expression.

"That's Lady Cynthia, Lord Thorpe's fiancée," Lucy told her cousin, a rather waspish note entering her usually lilting voice.

"Fiancée!" Jennie choked, whirling to look at her cousin in astonishment. "Doesn't that rather depress your ambitions? I mean, it isn't as if the man is free."

"It does lend a bit of challenge to the thing, doesn't it?" commented Lucy irrepressibly. "I merely told you I was going to marry the man. I never said it was going to be easy."

Jennie was about to question Lucy further, perhaps even intending to try to drum some sort of sense into the widget's head, when a movement in the previously empty box a quarter of the way around the level theirs was situated on effectively robbed her of coherent speech. "Well," she snapped, when her voice at last returned to her, "if that isn't the most odious thing I could ever have imagined!"

Lucy looked at her strangely. "I don't think it's

quite that bad, Jennie," she told her cousin sourly.
"After all, did I rake you over the coals when you
told me about your Kit? I thought you'd stand
my ally in this, cousin, really I did."

"Oh, no, Lucy!" Jennie interrupted hastily. "I
was not condemning *you*, truly I wasn't. It's just
that I just caught sight of Kit entering that box
down there. No! Don't look now for pity's sake, I
think he might have seen us. He's got Mr. Ives
and Mr. Norwood with him."

"Don't you wish to see those gentlemen?" inquired Lucy, still not seeing anything too out of
the ordinary in the whole affair. "I quite like
Ozzy myself, though I can't say I'm terribly fond
of Mr. Ives. Why not leave Aunt Rachel here and
trot on down to visit with them before the first
act?"

Jennie spoke through clenched teeth. "Because
they have three of those opera dancers you said
he didn't have in keeping with them, that's why!
Oh! The nerve of the man! Just because I have
been avoiding him he thinks he can parade about
town with some . . . some *lightskirts*. Didn't he
know I'd be here tonight? How could he do this to
me, Lucy? Has the man no sense of decency?"

"He might have, Jennie," replied Lucy realisti-
cally, "although I cannot actually speak for the
man, not having ever been that closely acquainted
with him; although his being an officer predis-
poses anyone to assume he is also a gentleman,
doesn't it? As to *how* he dared to do the thing, I
believe the answer might just lie in the fact that
you haven't spoken a single word to the man in a
week and he had no idea you would be attending
the theater tonight with me. Now really, dear,
keep your voice down or you'll wake Aunt Ra-

chel, a development I'd much rather avoid, as the woman has this infuriating habit of asking entirely the right questions. Now, now," Lucy pressed, seeing Jennie's woebegone expression, "don't go into a taking. After all, it isn't the end of the world."

"Don't worry about me, Lucy," Jennie returned, rallying. "I shan't weep millstones over that beast. Oh, I admit to having been a trifle cast down momentarily, but I have no plans other than to stay here and enjoy the play. And I'll be dashed if I'll sit and stew just because my husband chooses to display his lack of good taste in public."

Jennie's splendid recovery earned her Lucy's deep admiration, and that recovery lasted all the way to the end of the second act of *The Clandestine Marriage*—a story concerning the marriage of a rich, vulgar cit to a bored lord of the realm who openly hated the cit. The cit, it evolved, couldn't have cared less, just as long as her marriage meant she could go to court.

Was that how Kit saw her? Jennie questioned in her agitation. Did he think she saw him as a stepping-stone into society? Is that why he felt it was reasonable for him alternately to use her and then discard her, only to parade about in public with loose women to show his disdain? Well, the Countess of Bourne thought, I do believe Lord Bourne is sadly out if he thinks he can depress my pretensions to "society" that easily. But before I can hold my head up in that society I must rid him of the idea that he can continue on with his ladybirds so publicly.

"Lucy," Jennie purred sweetly to her cousin as the curtain fell, "I have just had the most happy notion. I believe I shall make use of this timely intermission to pay a visit upon my husband in his box." Rising from her seat, Jennie stepped carefully around the slumbering Aunt Rachel and looked back at her cousin. "Are you coming, Lucy?"

"You must be joking!" Lucy chuckled, a broad smile lighting her features. "I wouldn't miss this for the world! I vow it will be famous, absolutely famous!"

Kit was not a happy man, and he hadn't been one for a long time—ever since the morning he had stood gazing out over Berkeley Square trying vainly to figure out how a nice fellow like himself had ever gotten into such a mess as this. So complete and permanent had been his rapid descent into the doldrums that Ozzy, always out to do his possible when it came to his friends, had decided to take desperate measures. To Ozzy, desperate measures meant Mademoiselle Yvette de La Fontaine, Drury Lane's latest answer to the Englishman's love of "finest French pastry." Too fatigued to enter into an argument with his well-meaning friend, Kit agreed to accompany Ozzy and Dean to Covent Garden, La Fontaine and two of her friends from the chorus making up the remainder of the small theater party.

The actress, dressed to within an inch of outright ridiculousness, and smelling to high heaven of some heavy French scent, seemed to think she had reached the very pinnacle of success in being seen on the arm of the wealthy, handsome Earl of Bourne and planned to make the most of the evening. Hanging daintily from his lordship's arm ever since the Bourne carriage had picked them up from their temporary quarters in Clerkenwell, La Fontaine had worn a dreamy smile brought on by visions of the jewels and furs the earl would shower on her once he had established her in a discreet love nest somewhere on the near fringes of Mayfair. So intense was her absorption in her dream that she did not notice that the earl was paying next to no attention to her.

While Kit sat mute in his seat, variously wishing it were Jennie who sat by his side and wondering if it might still be possible to rejoin his regiment and die a heroic death in action, Ozzy, feeling very full of gallantry and good spirits at his coup in getting Kit into company once again, took an inventory of the occupants of the nearby boxes. The house was full tonight, he noticed idly, with all the world and his wife out to see the play and be seen. There's a good looking yeller-haired wench, he remarked idly to himself before, suddenly sitting up very straight in his chair, he exclaimed: "Good God, man! Kit, look over there a moment. It's your wife—and looking fine as ninepence, if I do say so myself."

Kit's ennui disappeared instantly, and he leaned forward just in time to see his wife turning back toward Lucy Gladwin—too late to see the look in her eyes, but definitely in time to see the stiffness of her spine and the bright flush of color running up her neck. "This'll set the cat among the pigeons," he muttered under his breath before saying more loudly and with every intention of lacing his speech with a languid drawl, "So it appears, Ozzy. What of it? Lucy's aunt is with them, so they're adequately chaperoned. Do sit back, man, else you'll fall into the pit and Celeste there will have to endure the play without your services as interpreter."

Ozzy, never known for his quick wit, was still

sufficiently up to snuff to know having your wife
and your latest flirt under the same roof—even a
roof so large as that of Covent Garden—was not
exactly a sought-after experience. While marvel-
ing at Kit's show of unconcern, Ozzy was much
more impressed with Jennie's behavior, as he
was sure she had seen them by now. "Like that
girl excessively, you know," he approved aloud,
turning in his seat to look Kit square in the eyes.
"And you know what, friend? I don't think I'd
like it above half if you were to hurt her. Game
as a pebble, your wife, and it kind of damps one
to think she might be made uncomfortable because of your shabby behavior."

"You're becoming damned moral, Ozzy," remarked Kit sarcastically, "considering it was your
idea I accompany you here tonight."

Dean Ives, so far a quiet bystander in this
exchange, decided it was time to change the subject. It wouldn't suit his purposes to have the earl
and Ozzy at daggers drawn. Leaning across the
back of his own companion—rudely pushing her
drooping ostrich feather headdress out of the way
without so much as an excuse me—he endeav-
ored to engage the men in a conversation. "You
missed a most invigorating spectacle this morning, gentlemen. A few friends and myself went to
Holburn to view a badger being drawn in a
menagerie there. I must say, those places employ
the most extraordinary-looking people. I wonder,
Kit, these servants of your lady wife's—do you
think any of them came from there? I know
you have a giant and a dwarf. Do they do tricks,
d'you think? I say, perhaps they juggle?"

"How would you like to juggle your front teeth?"
Kit inquired pleasantly enough, effectively put-

ting an end to the discussion, and it was difficult
to tell just who of the party was most grateful
when the curtain rose on the first act.

When the curtain fell again Kit chanced a quick
peek in the direction of the Gladwin box, just in
time to see his wife departing through the door
at the rear. Where the deuce could she be going?
he thought angrily. And unaccompanied as well.
But no, there goes Lucy, trailing behind her like
some grinning idiot off to see the fair. What
maggot can Jennie have taken into her head
now?

Kit did not have long to wait for his answer, if
he had only been paying attention, as there soon
came a knocking on the door of the Norwood box.
When Ozzy, having detached himself from his
clinging feminine companion with some difficulty,
at last opened the door, it was to see Lady Bourne
waiting without, Lucy Gladwin standing behind
her, smiling and waggling her gloved fingers at
him. "Well, Mr. Norwood, have you been somehow transformed into marble?" Jennie asked, tilting her head inquiringly.

"Lady Bourne!" Ozzy squeaked, his voice climbing octaves he thought he had left behind at the
age of thirteen. "Do you really think . . . I mean,
that is to say . . . oh, ma'am, are you really
sure . . ."

Jennie put the man out of his misery. "My
husband, Mr. Norwood. Is he not within?"

Ozzy could only nod, his voice now having completely deserted him.

If Jennie had been in better spirits she might
have felt her tender heart moved by Mr. Norwood's plight. But she was feeling sorely tried at
the moment, and her charity was all directed

toward herself. Her features hardening slightly, she looked the uncomfortable man straight in his anguished blue eyes and pushed pointedly: "Then perhaps you will have the goodness to step aside and allow us to enter."

Kit had been deep in his own thoughts and was therefore guilty of paying little attention to what had been going on at the door, but when he saw his wife guiding her skirts through the narrow opening he immediately knew what it was like for a drowning man to see his entire life flashing past his eyes in an instant.

"We have the guests!" La Fontaine lisped delightedly, being none too intuitive and not feeling the sudden chill that had descended on the box. "Will none of you fine gentlemen make us the—how you say—introductions?"

Refusing to give Jennie the satisfaction of seeing how much she had discomfited him, Kit rose and bowed to the newcomers. "How remiss of me. Of course you must be introduced. Ladies, this charming woman is my wife." He then went on with the more formal, detailed introductions, steadfastly refusing to look directly into Jennie's eyes to see the hurt he was sure was lurking there.

That Jennie was hurting was not an exaggeration. But if Kit believed that Jennie was about to let him or anyone else know it was killing her, absolutely killing her, to see her husband sitting so comfortably next to that obvious lady of the evening, they were sadly out. "You are French, Mademoiselle de La Fontaine?" she said brightly once the introductions were complete. "How marvelous. It has been an age since I've had anyone to practice my rather lamentable schoolgirl French on—do you mind?" Not waiting for an answer,

she launched into a cheerful monologue touching
lightly on the weather, the play they were seeing
that evening, and the oppressive crush of people
in the lobby clamoring for lemonade during the
intermission, all conducted in flawless French.

Looking faintly dazed by this flurry of words,
La Fontaine—who had been born and raised
within spitting distance of Piccadilly—frowned
intently, tilted her head to one side in deep
thought, and then replied brightly, *"Oui!"*

Jennie clapped her hands in seeming delight.
"Quite right, mademoiselle!" she trilled. Then
leaning down more closely to the seated woman,
Jennie delivered the *coup de grace.* "Mademoiselle," she said almost gently, *"savez-vous que
vous aver le nez d'un cochon?"*

Ozzy, who had been taking a restorative sip
from the silver flask he carried with him in case
of emergencies, started violently, felt a bit of the
fiery fluid slide down his throat improperly, and
could not resist a fit of coughing that had people
from several of the nearby boxes looking to see
just who was dying.

It did not help Ozzy's sensibilities overmuch
either when La Fontaine, totally uncomprehending
that Lady Bourne had just remarked that the
actress had the nose of a pig, only smiled va-
cantly and said, *"Merci, madame,"* before sitting
back complacently to push at the curls in her
elaborate coiffure.

"Minx," Kit whispered in his wife's ear as he
decided the farce had gone on long enough and it
was more than time someone with some sense
took charge of the situation. Placing his hand
firmly beneath her gloved elbow, he steered her
neatly out of the box and into a corner of the
nearly deserted hallway. "What were you trying

to do, kitten, give poor Ozzy in there apoplexy? And you," he went on, turning to skewer Lucy with his accusing eyes. "I believe I have you to blame for most of this. Without your lamentable influence my wife would not have taken such a maggot into her head as to make a spectacle of herself by being seen in public with one of the muslin company."

"Why ever not, Kit?" Jennie cut in acidly. "It doesn't seem to bother you unduly, and you certainly have more consequence than either of us." Jennie would have said more, much more, but she belatedly realized that the vein in the side of Kit's neck was throbbing in agitation and she wisely subsided into mutinous silence.

By the time Kit escorted his wife and her cousin to their own box the intermission had been over for some minutes and they could return to their seats without being seen; but this was only after they reluctantly informed his lordship of their plans for the rest of the evening and promised not to blot their copybooks any further unless Lucy wished her father to hear of this night's work.

Once back in his own seat, the sullen La Fontaine, having unfortunately discovered just what Lady Bourne had said to her (thanks to Dean Ives, who had been only too happy to enlighten her), demanded to be taken home "toot-sweet," which suited Kit perfectly. But before he could make good his escape, Kit had to endure a few good-natured jibes from Ozzy. "I told you your wife was a rare right one, old fellow. Lead you a pretty dance, she will, and I can't think of a fellow more deserving of it, I swear I can't. Tell me, for I must admit to a great deal of curiosity—

what are you going to do now? Murderers hang, you know."

Kit's remaining store of humor—not a great amount—evaporated at the sight of Ozzy and Dean wearing such broad grins at his expense. "What happens now is that I escort Mademoiselle de La Fontaine back to her lodgings and then go on to meet my wife at the after-theater party she and Miss Gladwin plan to attend. As to what you two do, why, you may go to the devil for all I care, seeing as how it was your idea to come here tonight in the first place. If you recall, all I was looking for was some company at billiards at the Royal Saloon."

Looking down at the men with a fierceness that would give a charging rhinoceros pause, he said coldly, "I need not remind you that anything that happened here tonight will go no further. My wife is still so unknown in town that no one was probably aware she was even in this box tonight. As for Miss Gladwin, nothing she does surprises anyone, and I doubt the gossips will even bother to prattle about this latest ruckus of hers. Gentlemen, do I have your word?"

"Need you ask?" Ozzy responded, trying his best to look insulted. "Don't worry your head about us. Just go and do the pretty with your wife, old fellow. We'll take care of things here."

"Indeed yes," Dean Ives seconded. "It was ever so amusing an interlude, but you may rest assured, my dear fellow, that my memory is most adaptable. Anything for a friend, you know," he added ingratiatingly, thinking to himself that his lordship might put on a fine show of disliking his wife but deep down there was a good chance the man was besotted with the chit. Not that he could blame him overmuch, for the girl was a tempting enough morsel, but Mr. Ives knew better than to allow his heart to rule his head. So he kept these thoughts to himself, knowing they would not be taken kindly if he offered them as advice, and filed them away in case he should ever have use of them. One never knew what could be helpful to a man who lived by his wits, as did Mr. Ives.

The *ton* party already in progress in the luxurious townhouse located in Portman Square was, in its hostess's estimation, a roaring success, sure to be talked about as one of the grandest crushes of the Season. Of course the Season was young yet, actually only in its infancy, but Lady Kenwood knew she had set a high standard that would have her dearest friends gnashing their teeth when it came time to plan their own tame entertainments.

Jennie and Lucy, having arrived long after the receiving line had been dismantled, found it easy to blend in with the crowd standing about the fringes of the overheated ballroom where a sprightly country dance was in progress. This was Jennie's first real exposure to society, her experiences with local dances at home not able to hold a candle to this exhibition of rich surroundings and impeccably dressed guests. Indeed, if it hadn't been for the knowledge that Kit was soon to join them she might have been able to abandon herself to the enjoyment of the scene. As it was, she felt like a prisoner about to be led to the block, and her furrowed brow and rather fierce expression kept the gentlemen, more than a few of whom had decided there was a real beauty in their midst, to keep their distance.

It was left to Lucy to procure for them glasses of champagne, which she did with little difficulty, as she seemed to be on a friendly, first-name basis with nearly every gentleman in the room. It was likewise left to Lucy to keep up a flow of meaningless chatter, as Jennie had sunk immediately into the doldrums the moment she was sure Kit was out of sight. Unfortunately, when she did at last find her voice, it was to point out that Lord Thorpe and his two female companions had entered the room.

"Now watch this," Lucy whispered in her ear. "Lord Thorpe will deposit the chaperon with the other wallflowers lining the perimeters like vultures, dutifully dance this next set with Lady Cynthia, fetch her a glass of champagne before herding her back to her keeper, and then take off for parts unknown. Honestly, I can't fathom how the man expects to spend the rest of his life with that plain pudding—he can barely stand to do the civil with her now, and they are only betrothed, not bracketed. For an intelligent man, sometimes he seems as thick as a post. So what if Lady Cynthia is good *ton*? I'd wager my hope of heaven good *ton* never kept anyone warm at night!"

"Lucy," Jennie scolded, trying vainly to hide a smile, "you are incorrigible. Anyone who didn't know you would think you were horribly fast. Besides, it isn't like you to be so catty."

"Oh, really," shot back Lucy with a sly look. "And who was it, Miss Prunes and Prisms, who walked barefaced into a theater box containing her errant husband and three high flyers 'nice' ladies like yourself are supposed to pretend do not even exist? Besides," she ended rationally, "I

am not merely being catty or mean. I am merely
trying to save Lord Thorpe from himself."

"And *for* yourself?" opined Jennie, just as Lord
Thorpe, following Lucy's earlier predictions to
the letter, deposited Lady Cynthia with her chaperon and sauntered off in the direction of a collection of gentlemen who were standing deep in
discussion in a corner of the room. "There goes
Lord Thorpe, Lucy," she pointed out, "just as you
said he would. It seems you have been making
quite a project out of the man, if you know his
habits so well."

"Project?" her cousin parroted. "My dear child,"
she chirped, giving her dark curls a toss, "I
intend to make his lordship my life's work. Oh,
dear," she ended, taking in Jennie's startled expression, "I fear I shock you yet again."

Although her cousin's honesty was a bit unsettling, Jennie, being the sensitive person she was,
could hear the hurt that hid behind Lucy's flip-
pant speech. "No, you widget," she soothed softly,
"I am not shocked. I am, however, apprehensive.
Lord Thorpe is an engaged man. It would distress me greatly to see you disappointed, which
just may be the case this time around. Getting
your own way in matters of the heart is not as
simple as boxing Cousin George's ears to make
him stop pinching you every time your back was
turned."

"I know that, silly," Lucy agreed easily enough.
"But then again I don't want Lord Thorpe to *stop*
bothering me—heavens, I'd settle for making him
aware of my existence for a start. Then," she said
innocently, "we shall just let nature take its
course. Now, Jennie," she soothed, leading her
cousin to a nearby chair, "you just sit here and

wait for your gallant husband to drop off his actress and join you. I'll just toddle over there and see if I can't get Lord Thorpe's attention. Oh! There's Kit now—remember, coz, to keep your chin up. It wasn't you who was peacocking about with another man. Don't let him bully you!" And before the flustered Jennie could grab Lucy's hand—hoping her cousin's presence would keep Kit from giving her a bear-garden jaw in public— the girl was off, determined to take advantage of this opportunity of catching his lordship on his own.

Jennie watched Lucy until the girl disappeared in the crowd and then reluctantly turned to see if Kit had spied her out. Her stomach dropped to her toes as she saw he was even then advancing purposefully toward her haven in the corner, his handsome face looking quite unusually grim. Well, she thought, stiffening her spine, my conscience is easy. Let him try to berate me, just let him try, and I'll give him a piece of my mind. Who does he think he is, anyway—my keeper? No, her uneasy conscience reminded her, he thinks he's your husband—a thought that seriously under-mined her resolution to give as good as she got in the coming exchange of insults and re-criminations. Being a wife, she decided, letting out her breath on a sigh, certainly had its dis-advantages.

Kit could see the conflicting emotions chasing themselves across Jennie's face as he approached her through the crush of people racing onto the dance floor to take up positions for the deliciously intoxicating first waltz of the evening. Much as he still felt the lingering chagrin of having been made to deal with an enraged Piccadilly harpy's disgusting imitation of a French fit, he could not sustain his anger when he thought again of Jennie's masterful set-down of that same actress. Whether she was purring like a kitten in his arms or spitting like a lioness protecting her territory, which is how he liked to think of her attack on La Fontaine, Kit found that he was hard pressed to find a single thing about Jennie that did not appeal.

Coming up beside her, deliberately approaching her from behind, he whispered into her ear reassuringly: "If you promise to sheathe your claws, madam, I'm willing to convince myself that this is our first meeting of the evening."

Whatever Jennie had been expecting, it hadn't been this. Whirling to face his, to her mind, stupidly grinning face, she spat, "Oh, aren't you just! How very *condescending* of you, my lord, considering it is your own guilt you are willing to overlook. How very high-minded of you indeed! It must be that it is so intellectually elevating to be with a woman who speaks French. *Oh la la, monsieur*," she lisped mincingly, "you are, how you say, such a *pompous ass!*"

Kit accepted her biting condemnation without a blink, knowing he deserved all that and more from her. As for the impropriety of her appearing in his theater box earlier, he was already convinced she had suffered enough for that particular indiscretion and was not about to set her off again by bringing up the subject. Deciding that this particular battle did not matter so much as did the question of just who eventually won the war that had so far described their marriage, he merely bowed, saying, "Your trick, ma'am, I fancy," and then totally destroyed her composure by placing a hot kiss on the bit of skin that peeped from beneath the looped buttonhole of her kid glove at the inside of her wrist.

Jennie knew Kit was pitching it rather high, overacting his part in their little farce more than just a tad, but she was entirely too female to do more than stand back and enjoy his attentions while they lasted. Unfortunately, since her husband's intentions lay more with getting his wife alone in his bedchamber, he did not waste much more time in cheerful flirtation, but went straight to the problem that was foremost on his mind. Where was that incorrigible nuisance Lucy Gladwin, he asked his dreamy-eyed wife—who was still holding her wrist protectively with her other hand—so that they could corral her and her Aunt Rachel and hustle them out of here?

The earl's question brought Jennie rudely crashing back to reality. She had been so apprehensive of Kit's arrival, so sure he was to ring a peal over her head for her unforgivable behavior at Covent Garden, that the thought that their uncomfortable coolness to each other this past week had dissipated like fog evaporates beneath the warmth of the sun had effectively blocked her mind to Lucy's problems.

"Oh, dear," Jennie faltered, casting her nervous gaze quickly about the room. "I don't know where she is anymore. She was over there, trying to get Lord Thorpe to notice her, though I can't for the life of me see why, toplofty snob that he is, and engaged too into the bargain. But I can't see her anymore. Do you suppose she's off in some chamber or other crying her eyes out with disappointment?"

Kit snorted indelicately. "I'd find it easier to

imagine that it is Lord Thorpe who is hiding himself away behind a potted palm, his knees knocking in dread lest Lucy spy him out and make a cake of herself for his benefit. Blister it, Jennie," he said feelingly, "that girl has more brass than my Aunt Martha's favorite candlesticks!"

"She's in love, Kit," Jennie put in placatingly. "Or at least she thinks she is. I only hope she isn't about to suffer a sad disappointment of the heart."

"She ought to suffer a stinging pain in her hindquarters, administered by that harum-scarum father of hers who should have taught her better," Kit said authoritatively. "Thorpe is one damned officious so-and-so, although I grant he's known as a true Corinthian, at home on turf or table. Actually, I imagine he'd be tolerable, if he didn't have such a fine opinion of himself. Not that I have ever had much to do with him—his set is older, you know. But from all I've observed of the fellow, rank, fortune, and lineage are all that concern the chap. Even his marriage, I've heard, was arranged more for its blending of blue blood than anything else. Why, Lucy has about as much chance of snagging Thorpe as she does of turning her flea-witted father into the Dean of Cambridge. Don't frown, kitten, it's not as if you don't know I'm right."

Of course Kit was right, not that it hurt Jennie any the less to hear it. But she had no time to tell him this, as she could at last see the diminutive Lucy off in the distance, engaged in conversation with not only Lord Thorpe but Lady Cynthia as well. Jennie tugged on Kit's sleeve and nodded her head in the small group's direction, and Kit turned just in time to see Thorpe's brutal dismissal of Jennie's cousin, executed with an insulting sneer, followed by the pointed turning of both his and Lady Cynthia's backs.

"That rotten bastard!" Kit was startled into saying, suddenly feeling quite protective of Lucy, who was even then blushing hotly at Thorpe's cold dismissal. "Come on, kitten, it's time we effect a rescue," he said from between clenched teeth. "I only hope I meet that bounder at Jackson's. How I'd love to get him in the ring and give him a sound drubbing!"

The Earl and Countess of Bourne, still largely unrecognizable to most of the company, made their exit from Lady Kenwood's triumph in considerable haste, cognizant of Miss Lucy Gladwin's trembling lower lip that warned of an imminent explosion—whether into tears or into a *faux pas* of immense magnitude, they were not about to linger to ascertain. Dragging Aunt Rachel in their train, they descended the broad staircase, and Kit signaled for his carriage and that of the Gladwins to be called for immediately.

While the aunt was bustled into her carriage alone, Lucy was led to the Bourne carriage, where Jennie plunged into a blistering condemnation of Lord Thorpe, Lady Cynthia, and the *ton* at large as she looked into Lucy's woebegone little face and saw the first crystal tears making their way down the girl's cheeks. "Don't you let those horrid people depress you, Lucy," she pleaded, holding the other girl's hands while Kit sat back in a corner, feeling about as useless as a wart on the end of Prinny's nose. "You're miles too good for either of them, you know."

It was disconcerting to see the normally bubbly, irrepressible Lucy Gladwin sunk to such depths of despair, and neither Kit nor Jennie could be brought to point out that she had brought her disgrace on herself. But, although down, Lucy was far from out, and so she said once her initial burst of tears had spent itself. "That Lady Cynthia and her missish airs don't depress me for a second, you know," she told her companions with some heat. "She is only digging her own grave by acting like some *grande dame*. It can only be a matter of time before Lord Thorpe realizes what a dull stick she is. It is just that I hadn't expected *him* to behave so cruelly. Why, he actually had the meanness to imply that we were never properly introduced and then turned his head away, cutting me dead."

"Arrogant jackass," Kit put in conversationally, earning himself a jab in the ribs from his wife.

"Oh no, Kit," Lucy protested, still intent on protecting the man. "He cannot help that he was raised to believe he is the greatest thing since the invention of fire! There is a wonderful man beneath that air of superiority—I just know it."

"Of course there is," Jennie agreed unconvincingly, secretly believing the only thing that could ever force any common sense into his lordship's handsome blond head would be a heavy, blunt object.

"Of course," Kit echoed, a small bit of humor entering his voice. "The question remains, though, ladies, why anyone could possibly care enough about the fellow to take the time to dig for it."

The carriage pulled to a halt behind the Gladwin equipage, and Lucy was forced to keep her rebuttal for another day. Once she was gone, Kit slid an arm around Jennie's shoulders and pulled her more closely against his lean frame. "Now, isn't this cozy?" he asked, breathing into her curls as the carriage moved off toward Berkeley Square.

Chapter Ten

It was a miracle the two of them were even
speaking to each other. Heaven only knew Jennie had a full budget of woes, thanks to Kit; and
his life had not exactly been a bed of thornless
roses since her advent into it. But they were both
young, both strongly attracted to each other, and,
at this comfortably romantic time of night, disposed to putting their squabbles aside for the
moment and simply enjoying the fact that, for
the moment at least, they seemed to be in harmony with each other. Youth had many draw-
backs, but the ability to adapt readily to most
any situation certainly couldn't be termed one of
them.

So it was a conspiratorially merry pair that
ascended the stairway of the Bourne mansion
shoes in hand, alternately giggling and shushing each other as they made their way to the
master bedchamber, Kit pushing up the tip of
his aristocratic nose and oinking under his breath
and Jennie giggling behind her hand as she
pleaded half-heartedly for him to stop being such
a goose.

It was only once they were in Kit's chamber,
the door safely closed behind them, that Jennie
began to feel the first tremors of uncertainty.
She had been here before, as if she could forget,

and even now, even with her feelings running so deliciously high, she was not quite sure that she should be here again. Each time they had been together it had ended badly. So why was she taking yet a third chance at heartache?

Kit could sense Jennie's sudden reluctance, even as he was mentally stripping her of her lovely evening gown and planning his strategy meant toward getting her into his bed with as little fuss as possible. "What's amiss, kitten?" he asked, trying for normalcy. "If you're worried about undoing that long line of buttons marching up your back, never fear. I am more than willing to act the lady's maid for the evening. Don't be shy, kitten," he coaxed, smiling as he walked toward her. "I promise to close my eyes if that's what's bothering you. I am nothing, you see, if not discreet."

Taking refuge in anger, Jennie sniffed and retorted, "Discreet, is it, Kit? Oh, aren't you just? That's pitching it rather high for a man who was just this evening cavorting about in public with that horrid actress. If you had an ounce of decency you'd be down on your knees begging forgiveness for your indiscretion, and not standing there grinning like a bear and trying to get me into your bed!"

Jennie's plain speaking effectively doused Kit's ardor, and conversely ignited his temper. "You picked a plaguey queer time to be splitting hairs over which of us was indiscreet, madam. *I* did no more than any man, single or bracketed, has ever done. It was *you*, my dear, who set a precedent tonight by making a public scene the likes of which would put Caro Lamb's worst folly in the light of a schoolgirl prank." Considering the fact that Caro Lamb had been said to have once

danced naked on a dining-room table in front of a
roomful of titled gentlemen, that *was* really pitching it rather high, and Kit knew it the minute
his words were out. But, he could see, the damage was already done. Jennie's lower lip began to
tremble, and it looked as if she was about to
break into tears.

But Jennie did not cry, although she was sorely
tried not to burst into tears at Kit's unfair insult.
It took her a moment or two to get herself together, but in the end she tilted up her chin and
decided to state her position once and for all and
then walk out of the room, head held high, never
to darken his lordship's door again. "It appears,
husband, you see me in the light of a resident
freak. After my behavior tonight, for which I
shall *not* apologize, I may just agree with you.
However, I will not take this blame alone. Did it
never occur to you that I was left to fend for
myself in London, having never been offered any
assistance from you? And what is a great deal
more to the point," she went on, clearly extremely
incensed, "I believe I have managed extremely
well on my own, having assembled a staff and
found someone of good standing who agreed to
shepherd me about London whilst my erstwhile
husband was off behaving like a mongrel dog
who had slipped his leash. So don't you tyrannize
over me, Kit Wilde!"

Jennie in a heat was a treat to Kit's eyes, and
he almost made the fatal error of saying so. Instead, common sense intervened and he struck a
pose of husbandly penitence. "It *was* my fault
that we had such an unfortunate incident tonight. I only went with Ozzy because he'd been
badgering me to accompany him. If I had only

known that you planned to attend the theater tonight . . ."

"You would have volunteered to drag me along like a good husband?" Jennie finished for him, crossing her arms over her chest and allowing her slipper-clad toe to tap out a lively tattoo on the floor.

Kit had been a soldier long enough to know when defeat was inevitable. So realizing, he opted for a dignified surrender in the hope he would be allowed to keep his sword, as the saying went, and retain at least a semblance of honor. "I've neglected you terribly, haven't I, kitten," he soothed, gathering her into his loose embrace and stroking her back as a child strokes a favorite pet.

"You've been horrid," Jennie mumbled into his chest, not seeing any reason to dress the thing up in fine linen.

"That's my kitten," Kit said, a laugh rumbling deep in his chest, "not drawing in her claws until she's sure she's drawn blood. All right, sweetings, I've been horrid. But am I completely beyond forgiveness? Even if I solemnly promise to mend my ways? After all, I haven't been so bad, have I? I haven't cut up nasty about Montague once since he took that cleaver to me. And didn't I only cuff Del's ear for copping my gold watch the other day, when I could just as easily have tossed him out on his dishonest rump?"

"He said he was only keeping his hand in, so to speak," Jennie protested feebly, "so as not to get rusty."

Kit knew Jennie was weakening, and he immediately took advantage of the situation, slowly maneuvering them toward the wide bed as his hands made short work of the line of covered buttons that represented his last barrier to her capitulation. "Of course he was, kitten," he concurred easily, nuzzling her ear with his warm, talented lips. He had her on the coverlet now, and by the way her soft arms were encircling his neck, he was certain that this evening would have a more than satisfactory conclusion. Nothing, he mused self-satisfyingly, was so bad that a little lovemaking couldn't make it right.

There came a sudden knock at the door, followed by the sound of a low-pitched argument going on in the hallway. Kit muttered a violent oath and rolled over onto his back, searching his memory once again for some sin he had committed that he was being tortured this way. Recognizing Miss Bundy's voice, he called out, "Bundy! What in thunder are you about out there? Can't a man have a little peace in his own bed?" The inadvertent double-entendre caused him to chuckle a moment before his temper regained the upper hand. "Damn it, woman, speak up! You were loud enough before."

Being no more pleased by the interruption than her husband, Jennie was still quicker than he to realize that Bundy would not disturb them unless something very important was happening. Struggling back into her gown, which gaped badly now that its buttons were all undone, she scrambled off the bed and opened the door. "This had better be good," she gritted between clenched teeth, surprising herself by realizing she was feeling more than a little deprived at being interrupted.

"Oh laws," Goldie whined from her position slightly to the rear of Miss Bundy. "I knowed it was wrong ta bother his lordship when he was frolickin', and so I told Miss Busybody here."

Miss Bundy, who did not look lightly upon being termed a busybody, was quick to put an end to the maid's lamentations. "Goldie," she said with a hard edge to her voice, "you haven't the wit of a flea. And it's not as if there were anything else to do, what with the tweeny bawling like a sick calf and calling for Miss Jane."

Jennie deciphered enough of this interchange to realize that Charity, that poor dear thing, was the reason for this late-night intrusion. "What's wrong with Charity?" she questioned the agitated Miss Bundy, drawing the woman inside and closing the door on the teary-eyed Goldie. "Did she have a bad dream?"

Miss Bundy's exacerbated nerves did not need this naive assumption to push them beyond the point of no return. Having had Jennie in her charge since the girl was in soggy drawers, Miss Bundy now addressed the grown woman as if she were still a child. "Is she having a bad dream? If that isn't foolish beyond permission—as if I wouldn't know how to deal with such a thing without banging down his lordship's door in the middle of the night. No, she is not having a bad dream. The chit *is* a bad dream, and now she's about to do just what I warned you she would do when you took her in. She's about to, er . . ." And here Miss Bundy's resolve deserted her, seeing as how the earl, wrapped now in his maroon dressing gown, was standing there staring at her as if she were the oddest creature in the world.

"What's wrong?" Jennie persisted, clearly perplexed. "What could Charity have done that's so upset the household? After all, she's only a baby."

Kit rubbed his nose and chuckled softly, shaking his head. "She certainly is, kitten," he concurred easily. "And it appears the baby is about to have a baby. Am I correct, Miss Bundy?"

The older woman, now looking as if she were about to have a spasm any moment, only nodded her head. "I know absolutely nothing about such things," she whined, wringing her hands.

"Yes," Kit smiled, taking the woman's arm and leading her out of the room, "I was reasonably certain that you didn't. Never fear, Miss Bundy, all shall be well. You just go wake Renfrew and tell him what's going on, and then you go back to bed. You look as if you need to rest a bit. Renfrew will take it from here."

Closing the door firmly on Miss Bundy's back, Kit turned to face his wife, his mind now firmly locked on the subject at hand—getting her back into his bed and taking up where they had left off when they were so rudely interrupted. But at the sight of Jennie, sitting on the edge of the bed and putting on her satin slippers, his brow furrowed and he was forced to ask her just what she was about.

"I'm going to Charity, of course," she answered civilly. "She needs me, I know she does, because she made me promise to stay with her when her time came. She's so dreadfully young, you know."

"And you're so very old?" Kit questioned, pushing her back down on the bed by the simple expedient of placing his hands firmly on her shoulders. "Renfrew will call in a doctor," he reasoned patiently. "I arranged the whole thing with him when I first saw Charity's condition. The doctor is probably on his way already. Besides, you're much too young to be witness to such a thing."

"Oh, stuff!" Jennie protested, removing his hands and rising once more to her feet. "If ever I heard a faint heart, it is you, Kit Wilde. I've seen kittens and puppies born a hundred times. There can be little difference between the species."

Kit smiled evilly. "I don't know about that, sweetings. If Charity has a litter, though, I'll be the first to admit to your reasoning." His handsome face hardened when he realized that Jennie was serious; she had every intention of being a witness to the birth. Grabbing her elbow as she made her way purposefully to the door, he acknowledged her loyalty but at the same time insisted she listen to reason. She had no place in any room where a birth was about to take place. A *conception*, he mused to himself without so much as one single pang for his selfishness, was quite another matter!

Looking down at Kit's hand, her expression telling him that she was not best pleased to see his fingers still clutching her person, Jennie told him coldly, "You can either detach that hand, my lord, or grace us with your presence in Charity's room. These affecting demonstrations meant to impress on me the delicacy of my station do nothing but highlight your own self-interest. Now," she ended regally, "I suggest you either unhand me or prepare to witness the birth yourself, because *I am going to sit with Charity!*"

Kit was tempted, sorely tempted, to take up Jennie's challenge, but in the end his eyes slid away from her penetrating stare and his hand slipped from her arm. Jennie marched from the room with the look of someone going off on a mission of destiny, and Kit, desperately wishing there were someone about he could lay violent hands on and so rid himself of this nasty urge to crush something, stomped off downstairs to the drawing room and proceeded to get roaringly, messily drunk.

* * *

Jennie was spending the morning at home, having been kept up most of the night attending the birth of Charity's son, George, named after the Prince Regent, and not his natural father—a man Jennie had commented was anything but natural. Renfrew had been a brick through the whole thing, calmly ordering everyone about and then, once the hubbub was over and the doctor gone, taking charge of having the softly snoring earl carried to his bedchamber, very much the worse for the prodigious amount of brandy he had consumed.

Having given Renfrew the morning off, telling him he deserved a lie down in his quarters, and finding that Bob, Ben, and Del had deserted their posts in favor of the kitchen where Montague was busily whipping up some strawberry tarts, Jennie was forced to answer the knocker herself, which is the only reason she was now sitting across the tea table from the smiling Dean Ives. At their first meeting she had thought the man handsome, but closer inspection revealed the man's rather mean-looking, close-set, ice-blue eyes, and his looks fell off rather sadly once her own eyes concentrated on the man's single bad feature. Perhaps she was just tired, she thought charitably; after all, it wasn't as if the man had ever done anything to put her off.

"I'm sorry Lord Bourne is not up and about yet this morning," she apologized sweetly, pouring tea, and then making a great show of yawning behind her hand, "but we had a bit of a to-do here last night and the whole household is at sixes and sevens this morning." If she thought Mr. Ives would take the hint and cut his visit short she soon saw that she had sadly mistaken her

man, for he merely nodded his understanding
and then sat back comfortably, looking as if he
had every intention of taking up permanent residence on the red satin Sheraton chair.

"Yes," he said, looking at her quite oddly out of
the corners of his eyes, "I can imagine it was not
the most tranquil of evenings once you and Bourne
got around to discussing that little contretemps
at Covent Garden. But not to worry," he consoled
her, waving his hand negligently as Jennie stiffened in her seat. "I for one will not let it be
bruited about town. Besides, it was probably Miss
Gladwin, that bold piece, who put you up to it
in the first place."

"You are above yourself, sir!" Jennie shot back,
clearly intending to order the man from her house,
but she was not able to finish what she had
intended to be a thundering scold by Ben (his
mouth circled with white flour and bits of sugar),
who entered the room and announced that Miss
Gladwin, that "right rum blowen," was without.

And so it was that Jennie had to content herself with giving Mr. Ives a look that would blister paint before rising to greet her cousin, whose
woebegone face served to drive anything but concern for the other girl out of her mind. "Lucy,
pet," she commiserated, drawing the girl down
beside her on the settee, "you're looking burnt
to the socket. It was I who was up all night, not
you."

While Jennie and Lucy held hands and whispered under their breath, totally ignoring the
man who should have had enough sense to excuse himself from this intimate family gathering, Dean took the time to observe the pair and
adjust his ideas accordingly. He had thought Jennie to be an easy touch, but she had shown him

that she could be a cool hand when one of her
own was attacked. Indeed, if that hellcat Gladwin
chit hadn't shown up so conveniently he knew
he'd be out on his ear by now, no doubt with a
sound admonition never to darken the Wilde door
again. Since that possibility did not at all suit
his plans for staying close as sticking plaster to
the young, wealthy earl and his beautiful wife,
he immediately set about the task of making
amends for his verbal *faux pas*.

He tried flattery first, thinking to work his
way back into the countess's good books by wax-
ing almost poetic over the beauty of Miss Gladwin's bonnet; but when Lucy merely wrinkled
her nose and said, "What, this old thing? Are you
losing your eyesight, Mr. Ives?" he knew that
Lucy at least was too smart to let fine words cut
any wheedle with her, and he once more retired
from the field but, unfortunately for the ladies,
not from the premises.

Jennie had the softest heart in creation, but
she became a tiger in the defense of her friends,
and therefore she felt not a single qualm as she
persisted in whispering to Lucy, pointedly ex-
cluding Mr. Ives from the conversation. Wilde
has the devil's own luck, that neglected gentleman was left to think, filling his ice-blue eyes
with the sight of an animated Jennie describing
the wonder of Charity's new son. From his observation last night at the theater, Mr. Ives felt that
his lordship had deep feelings for his bride, no
matter how sadly he neglected her, and he wondered if that affection could be turned to his own
advantage.

As this new train of thought interested him to
the exclusion of milking whatever he could from
a ridiculous conversation consisting mostly of ex-

clamations about the tininess of infant finger-
nails and the softness of infant skin, Mr. Ives
stood, bowed gracefully from the waist, and took
his leave, an action that caused Jennie to mutter
feelingly, "One can only hope he plans a pro-
longed sojourn to the Antipodes."

But the ladies were not to be left alone for
long, as Del, bits of sticky strawberry hanging
from his livery, soon arrived to announce that
Mr. Norwood, "that cater-cousin to the guv'nor,
is 'angin' about in the 'all, and iffen the pantler
don't get 'is arse ta anchor in the 'all soon there'll
be no tellin' who all will soon be 'ammerin' down
the door." His dire warning delivered, Del rubbed
a finger along the front of his jacket, licked the
gathered strawberry with his tongue, and turned
to depart, leaving Ozzy to ask what in the world
was a pantler, and did her ladyship know she
had thieves for footmen?

"Thieves, Mr. Norwood?" Jennie repeated coldly,
clearly taking exception to his bald statement.

Ozzy was nothing if not direct. "Thieves, my
lady," he insisted, grabbing Del just as he was
about to make his getaway. "I passed Mr. Ives in
the hallway and could not help but notice that
your footman here picked the man's pocket just as
he was going out the door. By the by, what was
Mr. Ives doing here, anyway? He seemed like a
man who had a lot on his mind—barely took the
time to say hello, and him that's known me any-
time these last three years."

"Mr. Ives was making a thorough pest of himself," supplied Jennie tersely, "which is a trait of
his you must be aware of if you have indeed
known him several years. What's more to the
point at the moment, however, is what horrid

thing he must have done to poor Del here to have the man revert to his former bad habits."

Del knew a champion when he saw one, and he made short work of pleading for his mistress's sympathy. "That queer cove never gived me no blunt fer 'oldin' 'is lily shadow or famlin' cheats, missus," Del whined piteously. "A man o' three outs, that's wot 'e be, so Oi jist sorta dipped me fambles inta 'is pocket-like, seein' as 'ow Oi be a dab at it, an seein' as 'ow ya said we wuz ta get tipped by all those 'igh an' mighty folk what's come 'ere. Don't send me ta Newman's Tea Garden, missus, like some Anabaptist."

" 'ere now," Ben admonished Del sharply, giving the smaller man a quick clip on the top of his head as the acknowledged leader of their small gang entered the room, having overheard the commotion from his station in the hallway. "Shut yer clapperjaw, ya fool. It don't do ta patter flash 'round the missus." Having satisfactorily dealt with his underling, Ben turned to Jennie. "Wot's 'e done, missus? We be birds of a feather, y'ken, but never there be no arch rogue or dimber damber among us. Wot's 'is be mine, missus, so iffen Del's gone an' got 'is bumfiddle in a sling, mine be there wit it."

"No pattering flash, you say?" Mr. Norwood put in, striving hard not to laugh out loud at both Del and Ben's cant language and the ladies' shocked reaction to it. Mr. Norwood could only surmise what their reactions would be if they understood even half of what the two footmen were saying, what with references to Newgate, Anabaptists, and a part of the human anatomy that females were allowed to sit upon but were otherwise admonished not to admit existed at all.

But Jennie was too overset to pay more than

token attendance to anything that had been said. Her primary concern was that Del had done what he had promised never to do—practice his pickpocketing talents on one of their guests. Never mind that Mr. Ives was not a valued friend of the family, and keeping the fact that he had cheated Del out of his earned tip to one side, Jennie knew that Kit would not allow such doings under his roof. Del would be tossed out into the street, and Bob and Ben with him, unless she could keep this little fracas from ever reaching her husband's ears.

Really, she thought uncharitably, all this fuss over the unpleasant Mr. Ives. It seemed incredibly silly to cut up stiff over what Del had seen as his right—taking the tip Mr. Ives had neglected to give him. "What did you get from Mr. Ives's pocket, Del?" she asked kindly, trying to marshal her wits about her before Kit, who had the most maddening habit of showing up just when he wasn't wanted, came on the scene.

"Not much blunt," Del answered, chagrined, showing off a few coppers that hardly seemed worth the risk of being caught in the act of putting his hand in a gentleman's pocket. "The cove must be laid up in lavender, missus, 'cause 'e sure ain't got deep pockets. All Oi got fer m'troubles is these coppers an' a tin tatler that don't even tick. An' this," he ended, passing over a slip of paper with some scribbling written on it. "Weren't 'ardly worth it."

Lucy, who had been considerably lifted from her doldrums by the footmen's shenanigans, came over and took possession of the scrap of paper. "It's an address near Holborn, and not a very nice one if I recollect my geography correctly," she said, squinting slightly as she tried to read the paper, which was quite smudged. "Whatever would Mr. Ives be doing with something like this in his pocket?"

"Nothing about Mr. Ives would surprise me," said a voice from the doorway as Lord Bourne, looking sadly out of sorts, sauntered into the drawing room. Ben, showing why he was the leader of his small band, quickly nudged Del, and the two hastily took their exit, fervently hoping that their mistress would find some way of explaining the scrap of paper without involving them.

The footmen were in luck, for Kit was too full of his own thoughts to spend overlong dwelling on insignificant matters. "I learned something about your Mr. Ives last night, from La Fontaine, as a matter of fact. I make free with her name, ladies," he said, bowing to Jennie and Lucy, who were trying hard to blend into the background, "because you and the lady in question have, thanks to my wife's odd sense of what is correct, already been introduced. Anyway," he pursued, turning back to Mr. Norwood, "it would seem your Mr. Ives is heavily dipped on his expectations. La Fontaine tells me he is nearly fully occupied nowadays in outrunning the duns. I thought I'd mention it, Ozzy, before he applies to you for a loan."

"That's mighty decent of you, Kit," Ozzy said, grimacing, "but I fear you are too late. He's into me for a monkey already."

"Whatever did Mr. Ives want with a monkey?"

Any remaining tension dissipated with Jennie's naive question. "Silly," Lucy laughed, hugging her cousin to her. "A monkey is sporting language for a sum of money—quite a considerable amount," she added with a quick look toward the blushing Mr. Norwood.

"Yes," that man concurred. "It would appear your man was right, my lady. Mr. Ives is indeed a man of three outs."

Kit, not quite understanding what was going on, translated. "A man of three outs is one who is without money, wit, or manners. Did Mr. Ives insult you, kitten?" he asked, more than ready to take umbrage. "I could do with a good punch-up."

Jennie assured her husband that she had not been insulted, merely bored to flinders by Mr. Ives's interminable visit earlier in the morning. "Really, it was excessively odd of him."

"Odd?" Lucy teased. "Perhaps you have acquired a beau. Oh dear, cousin, I do hope you will not allow your head to be turned by Mr. Ives's attentions." Lucy would have said more, but the earl's fierce scowl stifled the words in her throat.

"Lucy," that aggrieved gentleman said, "you're bidding fair to become a thorn in my side."

"Oh, Kit," Jennie protested quickly, "how very bad of you."

"Here, here," seconded Mr. Norwood. "That was very insulting, old fellow. Damned if I won't cut you dead when next we meet."

Jennie may have wanted Kit's attention diverted in some way, but to have her friends glaring at her husband as if he were the second most evil thing in the world did not suit her plans. "Montague has conjured up a fresh batch of his marvelous strawberry tarts, my lord," she sighed longingly, slipping her hand through her husband's arm. "Do you think you could ring for some? I have this overwhelming craving for one that I don't believe I can deny for much longer."

"A craving?" her cousin asked breathlessly.

"Never say, Jennie, that you're increasing. How utterly famous!"

If Jennie's try at diverting her husband fell a bit short of the mark, Lucy's enthusiastic exclamation certainly did not. Turning toward his wife as if she had suddenly sprouted a second head, he asked incredulously, "Are you, kitten? You never said anything."

"No, I most certainly am not!" denied his bride fiercely. "And I think it is beyond anything stupid how everybody is pressing me so. Only this morning my papa wrote asking much the same question. Really, if everyone is so set on having a baby around they'll just have to make do with Charity's infant." She then placed herself in front of her husband and mourned, "And you didn't even ask if it's a boy or a girl."

Relief, mixed with another emotion that seemed strangely like disappointment, spread through Kit, and he put his fingers beneath Jennie's chin and said gravely, "Forgive me, kitten. I stand before you agog with curiosity. Exactly what did Charity have—a little housemaid or a little underfootman?"

"Go ahead, Kit, mock me," she said imperturbably, "but I think it was famous, holding little George as he lay wrapped in his blanket. And he shan't be a footman for some London slavedriver either. I am already making plans to have Charity and her son sent to Bourne Manor as soon as may be. George is going to grow up in the country where there is plenty of fresh air and . . . and milk, and things like that." As this last was delivered in tones that warned that any contradiction of her plans would be looked upon as a personal insult, Kit only bowed his approval of the scheme and turned to ask Ozzy if he wished to stay and share luncheon with the rest of the family, adding that he naturally included Lucy in those plans. Mr. Norwood, mentally canceling his earlier intention of visiting his tailor to talk about an extra inch of buckram padding in the shoulders of his new puce jacket, agreed with some alacrity, smiling sweetly at Lucy and thereby giving Jennie to believe she sniffed a romance in the air. The subject of Mr. Ives, his financial state, and, fortunately for Del, the note that had been found in his pocket was dropped in lieu of talk of a more general nature, and harmony seemed once more to reign in Berkeley Square.

Chapter Eleven

Kit surprised Jennie by staying closer than sticking plaster all the rest of the day, declining Mr. Norwood's kind offer of allowing the earl to join him for settling day at Tatt's, Bourne saying that since Ozzy owed so much blunt thanks to his poor choice in racing nags, he would rather not be witness to watching a grown man blubber.

As for Lucy, that intrepid creature had only stopped by to tell her cousin that she had wangled an invitation to a picnic in Richmond Park that, rumor said, Lord Thorpe and Lady Cynthia were sure to attend. She wished she could have acquired an invitation for Jennie, but, she owned ruefully, it had been difficult enough to blackmail her friend Lady Standorf for the single one she had managed. Her aunt, that intrepid soul, was to chaperon her, Lucy told them, her eyes twinkling with mischief, so it would be easy as pie to slip away from her and somehow strike up a conversation with the love of her life. The wink Lucy gave Jennie on her way out the door gave Kit to murmur, "If I were more of a betting man I'd lay a few pounds on that vixen. If she ever gets the bit between her teeth, Thorpe doesn't stand a chance of holding out against her. I'd pity him if he weren't such a damned toplofty

bastard, if you'll pardon my blunt speech, kitten.
It's just that I've somehow developed a small
fondness for your cousin—odd, madcap creature
that she is."

"Papa says it runs in the family—coming from
my mother's side, you understand," Jennie told
him with a smile. "Bundy says Mama was also
considered an eccentric in her younger days. Something to do with her penchant for saving her
fellow man from the evils of gin."

"It figures," replied Kit laconically, his lips
twisting in a one-sided smile. "Thank goodness
you didn't inherit her Methodist ways."

And so it turned out, with their friends otherwise occupied and with neither of the Wildes
much inclined toward walking out that day, that
they somehow found themselves enjoying each
other's company for a leisurely luncheon, a restful
afternoon sitting about in the conservatory, and
for the entirety of one of Montague's superb dinners. It was only after he joined her in the drawing room that Kit began to feel restless and,
remembering an invitation to a friend's evening
party, he put forth the suggestion that he and
his wife make their formal debut as a couple.
"M'friends begin to tease me that all this talk of
my being bracketed is nothing but a bag of moonshine. It's time I get some of my own back by
showing off my pretty wife!"

After a full day of friendly camaraderie, this
plan for the evening suited Jennie right down to
the ground, and she readily accepted his invitation before he changed his mind. Calling for
Renfrew to have Tizzie please fetch down her
cloak, Jennie ran to the large mirror in the room
and did a quick inventory of her face and hair,

tucking a single errant golden ringlet back where
it belonged. Her gown, she knew from Goldie's
glowing praise and Bundy's tsk-tsking concerning the low cut of the bodice when she had first
put it on, was good enough to grace any hostess's
ballroom. Besides, hadn't Kit already commented
on how well the emerald-green silk complimented
her eyes?

Tizzie and Lizzie burst into the drawing room,
the former carrying Jennie's velvet-lined cloak
and the latter toting a small reticule that was
sewn in the same silk as her mistress's gown.
After wrapping the cloak lovingly about Jennie's
shoulders, Tizzie stepped back a pace and struck
a dramatic pose. " 'When you do dance,' " she
quoted in awful tones, " 'I wish you a wave o' the
sea, that you might ever do nothing but that.' "
Her recitation done, Tizzie swept her audience a
dramatic curtsy while Lizzie, the reticule hastily
stuffed under her arm, applauded lustily, verbally adding a "Bravo!" or two when her enthusiasm momentarily outran her shyness.

"That was truly splendid!" Jennie told the aging
actress sincerely as Tizzie rose creakily to her
feet. "I vow I am impressed."

"That was Shakespeare, kitten," Kit whispered
into her ear as he led her toward the door, "and I
vow I am about to be sick. Let's away before she
starts on Hamlet's soliloquy, as that would un-
man me entirely!"

Dancing was all right, Kit owned silently, if
one didn't mind prancing about like a trained
puppydog for all the world to see. All we need is
to wear ruffles about our necks and carry a red
ball in our mouths—he thought of himself and

his fellow males who had just lately been forced
to caper about the ballroom in a mad country
romp—and we would resemble a canine perform-
ing troupe. Thank the Lord that Jennie cared as
little for such tomfoolery as he did and had readily acceded to his wish to see what was about in
some of the other rooms. A good sport, that's
what his kitten was, he sighed happily.

"I will be your banker," Kit told his wife now
as he held out a chair for her and urged her to
take a seat at the round gaming table that was
one of a half-dozen or more that filled the small,
elegant salon just outside their host's elegant
ballroom.

"Oh," Jennie replied, looking up at him as he
prepared to take the adjoining seat, "we are to
play for money? All Papa used to allow was
matchsticks, and even then he beat me dreadfully."

"You've played faro before?"

"No-o-o-o," she admitted slowly. "Just a little
whist. Does that mean I can't play?" she ended a
little sorrowfully, preparing to rise to her feet
and surrender her chair to another.

But Kit assured her that although faro was not
usually considered a game for females, private
parties sometimes included a small-stakes table
such as this one. It didn't hold a patch on
Devonshire House, but then nothing much did.
While the rest of the company waited patiently,
Kit explained the rather simple rules for this
game that had accounted for the ruin of more
good men than every woman since Eve, and then
thoughtfully sent a servant to procure some liquid refreshment while he divided the betting chips
evenly between them.

Some call it beginner's luck. Others, those on

the losing end, term it as the devil's own luck. But no matter what name her fellow players chose to put to it, Jennie's luck that evening had Kit heartily wishing he could carry off dressing her in breeches and slipping her in the door at either Brook's or the Great-Go. A small crowd began to gather around as Jennie won draw after draw, making a shambles of the precept that in faro the odds always remain clearly in favor of the dealer. In a town so known for its love of gambling that Walpole had once remarked that he could not garner a teaspoonful of news in the whole city except what was trumps, word of Jennie's ongoing *coup* traveled quickly, and soon a multitude crowded into the small room, Dean Ives standing inconspicuously among the awed audience.

When at last Jennie tired of her easy victory, saying simply that she found faro to be tedious and boring, Kit stared down the remaining players who felt it a mite unfair to have the woman leave the table a winner and the two walked through the gaping crowd just as a waltz was being struck up by the indifferent orchestra.

"Oh, a waltz," Jennie sighed longingly. "Truly, this is the *only* dance that makes a whit of sense, without all that prancing up and down and separating from your partner for minutes at a time. How can anyone be expected to hold a civil conversation with a person who is forever tippy-toeing off into the distance?"

His pockets bulging with Jennie's winnings and his chest near to bursting with pride at her triumph at the gaming table, Kit executed a creditable leg to his lady, saying, "May I have the pleasure of this dance, ma'am, if you are not otherwise engaged?"

If the violinists were not of the first stare, and the conductor more than a little inattentive to the tempo, these lapses were lost on the young couple now gliding around the floor with eyes only for each other. So obvious was their enchantment that several romantically inclined dowagers were pressed to comment on it, while more than a few disgruntled bucks were heard to say they too could fall head over ears for a chit who had just very nearly broken the bank at faro.

Dean Ives, holding up a wall in the shadows near the dance floor, took the bucks' jealous jibes a step or two farther. The Countess of Bourne was lovely enough before winning so handily tonight. Now that appeal had doubled—not only for Kit, but for Mr. Ives as well. He smiled as he watched the earl wrap his bride carefully in her cloak before shepherding her out the door, thoughtfully tapping one long finger against his smiling mouth. Ah yes, the little blond countess was becoming more valuable with each passing day.

The moonlight coming through the window cast elongated shadows across the two figures who lay tangled amid the bedclothes on the wide mattress of the master chamber. The soft female sigh of contentment followed by a low, satisfied male chuckle were the only sounds to be heard, the rest of the house having all gone to sleep hours earlier. The night belonged to the couple snuggling close together under the satin coverlet, and they were making the most of it, with no intention of wasting a single moment.

"Listen!" Kit whispered, his soft breath tickling his wife's ear.

Reveling in the warm afterglow of their lovemaking, Jennie arched her throat so as to ease his access and questioned softly, "To what? I don't hear anything."

"Precisely, my love," Kit chuckled, raising himself on one elbow and playfully tickling Jennie's cheek with one of her golden curls. "No interfering Bundys, no birthing tweenies—just sweet, blessed silence. Even Lord Clive has consented to leave us alone. Perhaps people are at last giving the new Earl of Bourne some of the respect his lofty station entitles him to."

Jennie sat up straight in the bed, her movement toppling Kit from his position and landing him flat on his back. Clutching the covers to her breast, Jennie asked, "Lord Clive? I've never heard of the man. Who is he? Why would he bother us?"

"I knew it was too good to last," Kit muttered ruefully, running his fingers through his dark hair. "Me and my big mouth. You'd think I would have learned better than to speak my mind around you, my adorable busybody." Kit lifted himself up to plant a kiss on his wife's nose, robbing his words of any sting, but not diminishing her curiosity by so much as a single hair.

"Who is Lord Clive?" she persisted, holding the bedclothes tightly about her as, once her passion had been satisfied, her modesty in front of her new husband came bounding back full force.

"Right," the earl said, adjusting his pillow behind him and lying back against the headboard. "First things first. First Lord Clive, and then"—he smiled wickedly, waggling his eyebrows at her— "the seduction. Ah, kitten, you blush so delightfully."

Lord Clive, Kit told his wife while helping her plump up her pillow next to his, or, to be more

precise, Robert Clive, Baron Clive of Plassey,
was the man England recognized to be the founder
of the empire of British India. After distinguish-
ing himself in battle against the French, he had
eventually been made governor and commander
in chief of Bengal. But when ill health had forced
him to retire and return to England, his enemies
had accused him of using his offices in India to
line his own pockets. Parliament had impeached
him, and although he had eventually been ac-
quitted, his illness, added to his feelings of disgrace (and a rather sad addiction to opium), took
their toll, and the baron had committed suicide
in his home at number forty-five, Berkeley Square.

"And now his ghost is said to haunt the garden
in the center of the square," Kit ended, pleased
at the way his little tale had served to bring
Jennie back into his arms, where she shivered
deliciously at the thought of a ghost wandering
about among the plane trees and flowering shrubs
that filled the center garden.

"Is he an angry ghost?" she questioned, her
green eyes wide.

Kit placed a kiss on her curls. "No, kitten—not
that I know of, anyway. I would imagine he is a
sorrowful ghost; wandering about wringing his
hands—trying to reclaim his lost honor."

"How terribly sad!" said Jennie sorrowfully.
"Someone should do something about it. Try to
vindicate him, or something."

Seeing the light in his wife's eyes, Kit knew he
had to distract her, head her off as it were, before
she could build up a full head of steam, or else
there was no knowing what maggoty idea she
would take into her head as she set about wiping
the smut off Lord Clive's escutcheon. It wasn't as
if he didn't pity the man, but heaven knew he

had enough to deal with riding herd on Jennie's *living* projects, without trying to compete with a dead one.

"Well, puss," was all he said, sighing dramatically, "it *is* common knowledge that people will do very strange things for money. You should know, seeing as how you rode roughshod over your gambling partners tonight in order to gather in a tidy little fortune for yourself."

He had her attention now. "What fortune?" she asked, startled into sitting up again, this time without bothering to drape the covers about her bare upper body. "You said we were playing for tame stakes. And I only used one color chip— they were such a lovely shade of blue, you know."

"Those lovely blue chips were worth more than any other chip on the table, kitten."

Her eyes narrowed into slits. "How much were they worth, Kit?" she asked, a bit of steel creeping into her voice.

"Twenty pounds apiece," he answered her lightly, crossing his hands over his face as he pretended to duck out of the way of her soon to be swinging fists.

But Jennie sat stock still, mentally remembering how she had blithely thrown one blue chip after another, betting recklessly and then laughing in delight as the pile of pretty blue chips in front of her grew into a multitude. "How much did I win, my lord?" she asked, shutting her eyes tightly against his answer.

"Er . . . I . . . er . . . w-e-l-l-l . . . er . . ." Kit strangled, reluctant to say the words. But when Jennie held up her small clenched hand to within an inch of his nose and repeated her question he blurted out rather loudly, "Five thousand pounds."

"*Five thousand pounds!*" Jennie squeaked un-
believingly.

"Give or take a pound," Kit said and shrugged,
trying hard not to show his amusement at her
bewildered expression.

Jennie fell back heavily against her pillow,
muttering over and over, "Five thousand pounds.
Oh my Lord, *five thousand pounds!* Whatever
will I do with such a vast sum?"

Rolling onto his side, the better to slip an arm
around her slim waist, Kit crooned, "You could
always use it to hire a ship to send all your little
lost lambs across the sea."

His words snapped her out of her small spasm.
"Of course!" she exclaimed, sitting up once more
as Kit examined his now empty right arm and
muttered something unmentionable under his
breath. Him and his big, flapping mouth. Never
talk to a woman when she's between the sheets,
old son, he berated himself, else you'll end up
being jolted around like a jack-in-the-box without a moment of pleasure to show for the jostling.
Maneuvering himself upright again he began
kneading Jennie's shoulders as he dropped nib-
bling kisses along the length of her neck, trying
to bring her attention back to a more romantic
topic.

"The money was gained from gambling," Jennie told him as his lips traveled to her left shoulder before blazing a trail down her spine. "Therefore, it should be used for good—to benefit mankind in some way. Don't you see it, Kit?" she
asked, twisting in his grasp in order to face him.
"Our servants are all well to grass, living as they
do under our protection. But there are so many,
many more living in squalor all over London.
This money should be for them!"

Nuzzling Jennie's back provided sufficient stirring of Lord Bourne's hot, young blood to have him agreeing to house every London derelict under his roof. "Of course, kitten," he agreed, pulling her closer so that his lips could find the soft curve of her breast. "Anything you say, my love," he sighed, moving his head so that his searching mouth could narrow in on its delicious target. "Anything," he promised hoarsely, before the need for any more words was forgotten entirely and quiet ruled the night once more.

The Earl and Countess of Bourne woke the next morning at nine to refuse Goldie's offer of morning chocolate, and then spent the next hour satisfying quite another appetite before Kit remembered an appointment with his man of business and left Jennie to snuggle down beneath the sheets and go back to sleep. And so it was almost noon when the countess strolled into the drawing room and stood staring at a particularly unlovely vase with a look of utter rapture.

She went into luncheon when Renfrew requested it of her, but after watching her play with the food on her plate for several minutes Ben deftly snatched it from in front of her before it became entirely inedible. It was one thing, he told his fellow footmen, to eat up all the leftovers, but he'd be switched if he'd stand by idly and watch Montague's creations be turned into a whopping great mess of gray something or other by some love-struck ninny who couldn't be trusted to know a wax bean from a wax candle.

Still comfortably serene within her cocoon of happiness—for Kit had just that morning told her he actually believed he had fallen in love with her—Jennie wasn't even slightly put out when Ben entered the drawing room to inform

her that Mr. Ives, that "queer fish," was asking
to see her. "Send him in, Ben," she said serenely,
"and Ben, try not to judge others so harshly. We
are all God's children, remember. Show a little
charity, hmmm?"

"Yes, ma'am," Ben returned sagely. "But iffen
ya don't mind, Oi'll be keepin' m'blubber shut 'n'
m'charity ta m'self. That's a cove would take yer
eyeteeth, iffen ya catch m'drift, ma'am."

Mr. Ives spent the first five minutes of his call
in the usual mundane chatter about the weather
and how well his hostess was looking in her new
jonquil morning gown—which served to remind
Jennie of her former opinion of the man as being
a crushing bore. Oh well, she thought, resigning
herself to at least another quarter hour of insipid
talk, perhaps the poor man is lonely and in need
of company.

Dean could see by the glazed expressionless-
ness of Jennie's eyes that he was losing her, and
he decided to move directly to the point of his
visit. "I was witness to your great run of luck
last evening, my lady. After deciding to call today and congratulate you on your success I wondered if I'd find you at home or if you were
already out dashing about the town spending
your winnings."

If he had wanted her undivided attention he
had succeeded. Sitting up very straight in her
chair, Jennie informed him coldly, "I think that
is excessively bad of you, my good sir. While my
time spent at table last night was, I freely admit,
the greatest good fun, I am not the least bit
pleased to be saddled with all this ill-gotten booty.
After all, it is not as if I have the slightest need
for it."

The victim of this impassioned attack merely

sat back comfortably in his own chair and smiled. "I thought as much, ma'am, but I wanted to be sure I wouldn't be putting my foot in it to speak my mind on the subject." Seeing the spark of interest in her eyes, he wondered silently just how much of a bag of moonshine she could be made to swallow. "It would sadden you to know, Jennie—may I call you Jennie, seeing as how I feel I know you so well?—that there are an astounding number of homeless children in London, living a hand-to-mouth existence that would bring tears to the eyes of the strongest man. I most abominate speaking of such things to a lady, but I feel in my heart that you are sympathetic to the plight of these poor innocents." He had her now, he congratulated himself happily, for the moment contenting himself by heaving a sorrowful sigh and allowing a mask of sorrow to settle over his handsome features.

"Indeed, yes, Mr. Ives!" Jennie agreed eagerly. "As a matter of fact, Lord Bourne and I have already decided that giving my winnings to charity would be a praiseworthy resolution to the problem. But tell me, how is it you are interested? It pains me to say this, but I had not thought of you in such a light. . . . Oh, forgive me," she begged earnestly at his stricken look, "that was very, very wicked of me."

He waved her apology away. "No, no, Jennie, you have every right to question me. I know I resemble any other gentleman of the *ton*, racketing about town, seemingly without a single worthwhile thought to my name. But, I tell you honestly, I can no longer keep up the charade. I have run through my patrimony trying to help homeless orphans, and am even now deep in debt due to

my softheartedness, but it would never do to let
my friends know of my plight. It is only now,
speaking here with you, dear lady, that I feel
free to open my soul about my secret activities."

"I never would have thought . . . never mind,"
Jennie amended hastily. "Mr. Ives—Dean—it
would be my greatest pleasure to contribute to
your worthy cause. I won over five thousand
pounds, you know, and that should go a long way
toward easing the plight of those pitiful little
creatures. I do intend to set aside five hundred
pounds that I have decided to invest for my tweeny
and her young son."

Mr. Ives manfully hid his distress at this news
and plunged full force into his description of the
house he had set up to care for thirty orphans he
had personally taken under his wing. By the
time he finished, Jennie was more than agree-
able to driving out with him immediately to see
the little angels for herself. Kit had put forth his
low opinion of Mr. Ives, she knew, but that was
before the man had shown her this other side of
himself. Once Kit knew the truth he would see
why she was so eager to go with the man now,
her winnings tucked safely in her reticule. Her
tender heart felt dreadful about misjudging the
man, and, in typical Jennie fashion, she over-
reacted by giving him her complete trust.

Within moments they were on their way in
Mr. Ives's hired carriage, Jennie asking questions as quickly as they popped into her head—
wanting to know the names and ages of the
children she was about to meet, and if the women
who ran the orphanage were careful about the
regular use of soap and the absolute necessity for
vegetables in a growing child's diet. She would

have gone on, but as the scenery outside the carriage grew increasingly depressing and squalid she stopped talking and only stared, compassion wringing at her tender heartstrings.

Chapter Twelve

"Good afternoon, Bob," Lucy chirped happily, stepping inside as the footman opened the wide door of the mansion in Berkeley Square. "Is my cousin not ready yet? Do tell her to hurry, for, as my aunt made sure to remind me as I alit from the carriage, it would not do to let my papa's horses stand about in the breeze."

"Her ladyship ain't 'ere," Bob informed her, still engaged in a silent struggle to relieve Miss Gladwin of the glove she held tightly in her left hand. " 'ere now, give over, miss. Oi'll be givin' 'em back when yer off, promise. Ben'll 'ave m'bum fer a 'itchin' post iffen 'e sees Oi ain't doin' right by ya. It's yer famble cheats wot Oi'm apposed to lift, an' liftin' 'em's jist wot Oi'm affixin' ta do."

Lucy accepted Bob's explanation, hastily stripping off her left glove and handing the pair to him, asking worriedly, "What do you mean, Lady Bourne isn't here? We made arrangements to drive out together this afternoon in the Promenade. I have it on the best authority that Lord Thorpe will—never mind that. Where did she say she was going? When did she leave?" By now Lucy was sitting on the settee in the drawing room, her papa's prime bits of blood forgotten, and Bob, clutching the coveted famble cheats to his bosom, was staring down at her, his head awhirl with trying to remember all her questions. Dealing with the quality, he reminded himself for the hundredth time, was no lark in the park.

"Oi ken answer ya that, missy," Ben offered, sauntering into the room as if he belonged there. " 'er ladyship lopped off inna bankrupt cart wot that queer nabs Ives called up fer. Not wot Oi didn't caution 'er not ta go prancin' 'round town with the cove, ya mind. Gone since just past noon, they be, an' nary 'ide nor 'air of 'er since. Missus is a saint, missy, but there be times Oi doesn't wonder wot iffen she ain't awful ta let in 'er upper rooms, no offense meant, y'know."

Wrinkling her brow as she tried to puzzle out Ben's words, Lucy at last said, "She went out for a drive with Mr. Ives at noon in a—what was that you called it?"

"Bankrupt cart, missy," Ben repeated kindly. "Mr. Ives went an' 'ired 'imself one of them one-'orse chaises the cits keep fer Sundays so as ta put on 'oity-toity airs fer the neighbors."

Lucy nodded her head in understanding. "All right," she said, considering the evidence. "Lady Bourne decided to ride out with Mr. Ives, heaven only knows why, as I for one certainly do not. But they should have returned here long ago. Perhaps an accident?" she suggested, looking up at Ben for guidance.

"Or worse," returned the footman, recalling the tingling feeling he got at the back of his neck every time Mr. Ives was present. "Goldie tol' me as 'ow she fetched missus 'er winnin's afore she lopped off. Oi been askin' m'self wot a body wit five thousand pounds in 'er boung would be doin' ridin' inna bankrupt cart. Seems havey-cavey ta me, miss."

"I should say so!" exclaimed Miss Gladwin, rising to her feet and beginning to pace the carpet. "Now, Ben," she said severely, whirling to face the diminutive footman, "I want you to tell me everything—about the money, Mr. Ives, the whole of it. And in the very best English you can muster, please, Ben, as I think Lady Bourne may be in some kind of trouble. I'm counting on you, Ben; don't fail me!"

More than a quarter hour of valuable time was spent in listening to and then deciphering Ben's tale of what had gone on during Dean Ives's visit that morning, what with the agitated servant interrupting himself over and over to give Lucy a few pithy (and none too kind) interpretations of his own regarding Mr. Ives's character, disposition, and probable parents, as well as a few other breaks in his monologue during which time he roundly berated himself for not noshing that slimy cove on his noggin and putting an end to it before the missus could go off with him in the first place. But at last Lucy understood, and she immediately sent her papa's carriage, with Renfrew riding inside, off on a round of the clubs in an effort to find Kit.

Renfrew ran his master to ground at Watier's, and the earl, with Mr. Norwood in tow acting as interested observer, made short work of driving back to Berkeley Square. "Is she back yet?" an agitated Kit asked anxiously as he bounded into the drawing room, his eyes searching for Jennie. Although the trip from Watier's was not a long one, Kit had already been through several kinds of hell imagining what could have happened to his darling wife.

"She is not," intoned a gravely solemn Miss

Bundy, who, in company with Lucy and her Aunt Rachel, had been making great inroads on picturing Jennie in all manner of dire predicaments. "How dare that child tease me to death like this? I vow I feel like an afflicted parent, destined to spend the remainder of my days watching my head turn gray because of the viper I have nurtured at my bosom." Only Miss Bundy's sorrowful tone and very obvious distress kept Kit from telling the woman to stifle herself before he did her an injury.

Flying into a rage would, he knew, serve no real purpose—although it was hard to deny an almost overwhelming desire to kick something—and Kit purposefully downed a bracing two fingers of whiskey before asking Lucy to tell him everything she knew. Once the girl had delivered her small store of hard information—embellished more than a little bit by way of her fertile imagination—the earl knew they could have a real problem on their hands.

"Ozzy," he asked, "can you think of any reason for Ives to be calling on m'wife? I'd be inclined to think he asked her for a loan, but even Ives seems too intelligent to try such a ridiculous stunt."

Mr. Norwood could see that Kit was as sore as a boil and trying not to explode, and he could only hope that Kit wouldn't soon recall just who had first introduced Ives to the Wildes and take out his anger on him. "What? *Me*?" Ozzy exclaimed incredulously. "Why would I know anything? You know me, Kit, old fellow; dense as a house, that's me. I haven't a clue what maggot Ives has taken into his head. It's you that's got a brain sharp as needles. You figure it out!"

"You're a real brick, Ozzy," Kit gritted sarcastically as Lucy crossed her arms across her breast and rolled her eyes. "All right," he went on, taking a deep breath and squaring his shoulders, "I will figure it out. But," he warned, his fierce expression freezing Mr. Norwood where he stood, "once I *have* got it figured out I will expect your wholehearted cooperation in whatever steps have to be taken from there. Surely, old fellow," he drawled, "you are not so dull as to misunderstand what I am saying."

Ozzy swallowed hard and waved his hand as if to say get on with it. While the ladies sat watching from the sidelines, Kit took his turn pacing the carpet, telling everyone that he was sure Ives had fed Jennie some line of drivel that convinced her she must use her winnings to save some poor unfortunate chimney sweep or some such faradiddle. Perhaps, he told his assembled audience with more hope than assurance, once he had been successful in relieving Jennie of her heavy purse he would return her to Berkeley Square. After all, he pointed out logically, Ives couldn't kidnap Jennie, for goodness' sake—else he'd have to flee the country. "And God knows five thousand pounds isn't worth that," he ended, smiling a bit as he began to believe what he was saying. Jennie, sweet, gullible soul that she was, would be out her winnings, but she would have learned a valuable lesson about putting her trust in people who did not deserve it.

"Four thousand, five hundred pounds," Miss Bundy corrected helpfully. "Jennie quite naturally reserved five hundred pounds for Charity and little George."

"Naturally." Kit grinned, his spirits lifting momentarily. "But unless I sadly mistake my man, Ives will be paying his tailor and a half-dozen other creditors with the remainder of the proceeds. What I don't understand is why it is taking so long to relieve my wife of her winnings. It certainly didn't take Ives long to persuade her to ride out with him, if what Ben told Lucy is correct. No," he said, shaking his head, "there's something more to this, and I'd give my best bays to know exactly what it is."

The earl's bays were a real prize, and Ozzy saw his chance to have himself riding up behind them in his own curricle. "Ives has been running tame in this house before with you not home, right?" he asked in sudden inspiration. "Could it be your filly has bolted with him? After all, old fellow, you said yourself that she was an easy mark."

It took the combined efforts of Del, Bob, and Ben to keep the enraged Kit from bashing his good friend into a pulp, so great was the man's exception to the suggestion that his wife had run off with another man. "Now, now, guv'nor," Ben soothed as he dangled three feet off the floor, with his arms and legs wrapped around his lordship's waist and neck. "Anyone ken see wot the cove's dicked in the nob. Ya ain't gonna let no croaker with the wit o' three 'ave ya dancin' at Beilby's Ball?"

"What did he say?" Lucy asked Renfrew, who had by necessity become quite conversant in the footmen's mode of cant. "Ben has referred to Mr. Norwood as being crazy in the head, miss," he whispered under his breath as Kit peeled off his protectors and shook out his sleeves. "And then Ben suggested that his lordship shouldn't allow any foreteller of bad news who had only the combined wit of two fools and a madman to nudge him into doing murder and then being hanged. Beilby was a famous hangman, I believe."

"Oh," Lucy said, nodding her understanding. "Thank you, Renfew. Jennie said I could always look to you to know the answer to anything, and she was correct. Perhaps you have a solution to our current problem you might share with us."

"Well, miss, now that you mention it," Renfrew confessed shyly, "I have been thinking it might be a good idea to call in the Bow Street Runners and see what they think."

"China Street Pigs!" the three footmen shouted as one. "What d'ya want wit' them red breasts?" Clearly the Bourne servants had no high opinion of the gentlemen of Bow Street.

"The Runners would appear to be either extremely incompetent," observed Lucy's Aunt Rachel prosaically, "or quite the reverse, considering the reaction these servants have had to the butler's suggestion." As Lucy had told Jennie, her aunt might not be talkative, but when she said something it usually made perfect sense.

Kit's grudging acceptance of his hasty apology having eased Ozzy's fears that his lifelong friend was about to do him bodily harm, the man felt no qualms about opening his mouth yet again. "Bow Street would only assign one or two men," he said contemptuously. "If your lady is adrift in London with Ives it will take a small army to ferret her out."

Kit looked about the room, noticing the collection of bodies gathered around both doorways in an effort to hear what was going on, and then counted the heads of those already in the room. "A small army, hmmm?" He smiled, spreading his arms wide. "And what would you call this gathering, Ozzy? Look around you. What do you see?"

"I see a giant, a dwarf, a madman holding a

cleaver, two Drury Lane madams, and a trio of
bandy-legged escapees from Newgate. And all of
us, of course," he ended hastily when Lucy made
a point of clearing her throat to call attention to
herself.

"Oh, how famous," Lucy shouted, catching Kit's
drift in an instant. "We *are* a small army!"

Kit bowed her his congratulations. "My servants, you will understand, abound in all the
first-rate virtues—pocket-picking, petty thievery,
head-bashing, et cetera. Although my wife would
argue the point, I am sure, I believe it is time I
set my servants to a job for which they are
uniquely qualified. Gentlemen, ladies," he inquired
silkily, turning to the assembled servants, "what
say you? Can you find Lady Bourne for me?"

Ben smiled, revealing his sparse teeth. "Quicker
than the cat ken lick 'er ear, guv'nor!" he replied
promptly. "Jist let me an' the rest 'ave a little
council o' war, so ta speak, an' we'll be off."

"Report back to me here as soon as you learn
something," Kit called after the small group as
they headed for the kitchen to hold a conference.
"Lady Bourne may return on her own, you know.
But if she doesn't, I reserve the right of rescuing
her for myself. You just find her for me. Mr.
Ives," he said grimly, "is mine." At Tiny's groan
of disappointment Kit smiled at the giant and
added cheerfully enough, "Never fret, old son. If
you're very good, I just may let you have him
once I'm through with him," a promise which
resulted in a round of cheers from all the misfits
whose devotion to the angel who had rescued
them from poverty knew no bounds.

"What about me?" Ozzy asked, looking rather
crestfallen at the thought of being left out of all
the fun.

"You run around to Ives's rooms and see if you can pick up any clues from his manservant. Lucy and the rest of us will wait here in case Jennie comes home or . . ."

"Or what?" Lucy asked worriedly, coming over to Kit and laying a hand on his arm.

"Or until a message arrives telling us that Jennie is being held for ransom." Lucy gasped, and Kit wheeled on his heels, striding toward the library where he kept his pistols. He had gone through hell and more on the Peninsula, he thought ruefully as he lifted his pistols down from the shelf, but never before could he remember his hands shaking so terribly at the thought of a coming battle.

It was coming on to dark when Ozzy reentered the mansion in Berkeley Square, a note held in his outstretched hand. "Here it is, Kit," he shouted, tossing the paper to his friend before dropping heavily into a nearby chair. "I had the devil's own time getting Ives's landlord to let me in, but once I had crossed his palm with a little bit of the ready he became quite obliging. Ives has cut and run, that's for sure, as the whole place was stripped bare, and I found this note on his dressing table. I imagine he left it there knowing we'd be searching his place before long." Ozzy shook his head sorrowfully, obviously blaming himself for the whole affair. "I never knew what he was like, Kit, I swear it, or else I'd never have let him within sight of your Jennie."

But Kit wasn't listening. After reading the note he rolled it into a ball and angrily tossed it into the fireplace. "He doesn't tell us anything we hadn't already figured out once Jennie hadn't returned home for dinner. He's got her, sure as check, but the kitten's gambling winnings are no more than a down payment on the sum he's asking for now. What he doesn't say is how I'm to get the ransom to him—or when the exchange is to be made. That paper's as worthless as Ives himself."

Lucy could understand Kit's chagrin, for she felt just as helpless. She had been cudgeling her brain for the last hour and more without coming up with a single answer. But now the faint glimmering of an idea shed some light on the matter, and she jumped to her feet, crying, "What about the address Del lifted from Ives's pocket the other day? I remember it as being somewhere in Holborn. Perhaps it is a clue. Renfrew!" she called unnecessarily, for the butler was already making free of his mistress's writing desk, searching for a slip of paper.

"Ah, thank you," Lucy said, relieving the butler of his prize and handing the note over to the bewildered earl, who had not been informed of Del's little lapse into his former line of work. "We found this in Ives's pocket, Kit. See, it's the address of a house on Cow Cross Street. Surely this is a clue, for why else would the man have need of such an address if he did not mean to hide our Jennie away there while he waited for you to pay the ransom?"

Kit looked at the paper, hope leaping in his chest. "It may just be the address of some accomplice he has hired to serve him," he pointed out, trying not to become too excited. "A man can rent killers in Holborn at two a penny, you know."

"Jack Ketch's Warren, guv'nor," Ben corrected as he walked into the room. "That's the 'andle wot we gives ta Holborn. That's where the mis-

sus be, all right. But 'ow'd ya ken it afore Oi told
ya?"

The small army was back together once more,
and Kit readily allowed Ben to take charge for
the moment, everyone listening intently while
the thief-turned-footman painted a highly colorful picture of just what they were likely to find at
number fourteen, Cow Cross Street. All the houses
there were divided top to bottom into apartments,
most of them having two or more doors to the
outside, making them highly desirable homes for
thieves and other cutthroats. The house Ives had
chosen for stowing Lady Bourne in until his demands were met was one of the largest, housing
a gin shop on the ground floor, a gaming hall on
the first, and a half-dozen or more apartments
converted for use by low prostitutes. The rest of
the apartments, Ben informed them, were used
as dens for thieves and low toby men in the area.
" 'Tisn't a pretty place, guv'nor," Del added
unnecessarily.

By the time Ben was finished, Goldie was lost
to the small army, having been commissioned by
the earl to take charge of Miss Bundy, another
casualty, who had broken into loud sobs and been
asked to vacate the room before her hysteria
became contagious. That left Tizzie and Lizzie,
Renfrew, the three footmen, Tiny and Goliath,
Montague, Kit, Ozzy, Lucy, and Aunt Rachel. A
mixed bag of rescuers, but the best the earl could
come up with on such short notice.

Now they needed a plan. Ben took up his position beside Bob and Del as Kit stepped to center
stage and took command. After a few pointed
questions to each of his small assault force, during which he learned of their various specialties
and individual talents, he set about utilizing each

one of them to the fullest of their potential. The result was a plan that owed equally to ingenuity and good luck. It may not have done justice to Lord Wellesley's genius, but it was all they had. And, for Jennie's sake, they would make the best of it.

"And to think all this is happening because of a silly rabbit trap." Jennie shook her head as she commented ruefully on the bizarre chain of events that seemingly innocuous episode had set into motion.

"What's that?" Dean Ives, who had been consulting with his three cohorts, turned to ask, wondering if the girl had been unhinged by her abduction and taken to babbling to herself.

"Nothing that would interest you, Mr. Ives," she told him cuttingly, "as you don't stand to gain a groat by it. You know, of course, that this whole thing is no more than a great piece of nonsense. It would be famous if Kit refuses to pay you your blood money. Perhaps you should have thought of that before you began this little game. After all, Kit might not care a fig about me and refuse your demands. Oh yes indeed, Mr. Ives," she ended smugly, "I believe you just may have made a muff of it after all."

Ives came to stand in front of her, smiling down at his captive in amusement. "Oh no, my lady, I fear you are wrong there. I've seen your husband's face as he looks at you. He cares about you right enough, and I'll be willing to bet he'll pay me every penny I've asked for to have you back. I'm only sorry you have to be inconvenienced this way," he apologized, motioning toward the bonds that held her.

"No, you're not," Jennie contradicted.

"No," Ives laughed, "I'm not. I just thought it would be the gentlemanly thing to say."

Jennie would have given anything she had to be able to slap that silly grin from her captor's face; but her hands were tied securely behind her and she had to content herself with sticking out her tongue at Ives's back as he turned back to his companions. How could she have been so incredibly stupid, so trustingly naive, as to believe that farradiddle about Ives sponsoring an orphanage? Anyone could see the man hadn't a charitable bone in his entire body. Oh, Kit would roast her good for this one once he got her out of this terrible coil. That her husband would rescue her she had not the slightest doubt, only wishing that he would hurry because her surroundings, shabby, smelly, and dirty as they were, had begun to prey on her nerves. Imagine the many innocent children who were forced to live in such squalor, she thought worriedly. Surely such conditions could not be allowed to continue.

If Kit had known just where his wife's thoughts were heading, he would have made even greater haste in rescuing her.

It was full dark when Kit's small army descended on Cow Cross Street, their raggedy, unkempt appearances making no stir among the street's inhabitants. At a signal from their leader they dispersed, going off in small groups of two and three, while Kit himself melted into the shadows directly across from the front door of number fourteen, pulling Ozzy behind him.

"It's a good thing you convinced Miss Gladwin and her aunt that they'd serve no purpose coming here," Ozzy whispered. "Can't say as I'd like them to see what's going on over there." Kit looked to the open door of the gin shop to see two sadder examples of their fellow men as they staggered out into the gutter, a bare-chested female of indeterminate years pressed between them, sharing her wares equally with the men as they grappled drunkenly at her body.

"It's also a good thing Lord Thorpe's too high a stickler to have a reputation for taking Blue Ruin with his fellows in such places, or else we'd never have been shed of her so easily," Kit commented dryly. "But with Renfrew promising to keep them in Berkeley Square by brute force if necessary, I don't believe we'll have to worry about Miss Gladwin showing up to add her little bit to the rescue."

"She's game as a pebble, ain't she?" Ozzy remarked admiringly.

Kit pulled a face. "She is that, Ozzy, but I'll take my Jennie any day. They may both be full of heart, but m'wife's decidedly more restful. I don't know that I could stand Lucy's determined streak over the long haul. I tell you, Ozzy, it will take a strong man to keep that chit on the leash. Jennie may rule me, sport, but at least she allows me the illusion of being in charge. Take this mess with Ives, for instance. If it were Lucy hidden away in that building I'd be worried senseless wondering what scheme she was hatching in her head to free herself. Jennie, the sweet love, will remain calm, knowing it is my place to effect the rescue. It warms a man, truly it does, to know the love of his life invests him with so much trust."

Ozzy merely sniffed, thinking his friend looked more than a little smug, but he was not envious of Kit's good fortune, merely thankful he himself was heartfree and able to enjoy his women without having to feel responsible for them.

A movement from across the garbage-strewn street caught their attention, and Tizzie and Lizzie, a drooping Montague supported between them, came into sight. The former actresses were dressed to the teeth in matching costumes they had worn when portraying ladies-in-waiting some twenty years earlier, and their painted faces and outrageous plumed coiffures fairly screeched that these were two practitioners of the world's oldest profession.

Montague was a sight to inspire awe in his audience, which, thanks to the dramatic caterwauling of Tizzie and Lizzie, was growing by leaps and bounds. When Tizzie had produced the costume, Kit had known at once that it would come in handy, being, as the actress described it, "a suit o' clothes for a ghostie, picked up fer a song at a sale on Drury Lane." It consisted of a bloody shirt, a doublet curiously pinked, and a coat with three great eyelet holes upon the breast. A bottle of "genuine-looking human blood" was included in the sale, and Tizzie had made liberal use of the fluid, copiously dousing Montague's head and chest with the gory confection.

"Oh, good sirs, 'elp us please!" Tizzie cried as Montague moaned and lapsed into incoherent French. "We wuz set upon by footpads," the actress informed her audience, "and they 'ave done murder to Misyoor Montague. 'elp us, do, ta get 'im inside."

"*'elp us, 'elp us*," Lizzie parroted, allowing her low neckline to droop just a bit more under the strain of lugging the ample Montague toward the gin-shop door, and the sight of her buxom figure prompted three slightly built beggars to break from the crowd and offer their assistance to the ladies.

" 'ere now," said one of the beggars, a man covered head to foot in hideous running sores meant to illicit pity from passersby who would then drop pennies in his cup, "Oi'll 'elp ya, girlie."

"Hard to believe those sores aren't real," Kit commented, watching Ben take charge of the situation, Bob and Del assisting him as all five moved inside the gin shop and commandeered center stage by means of Montague's bloody appearance and the women's loud lamentations of woe and impending disaster.

" *'e's dyin', 'e's dyin',*" Tizzie screeched, ripping at her hair as Montague groaned and allowed his tongue to loll obscenely from the corner of his bloody mouth.

"Not 'ere, 'e ain't!" the tapster contradicted angrily. "Get 'im the bloody 'ell outa m'shop afore Oi finish the job wot the other coves started. 'ave 'im do is ruddy bleedin' somewheres else."

"Lizzie," Tizzie shouted loudly as the tapster moved to make good his threat, "show 'em the beans. Iffen they sees the lour mebbee summun will 'elp us fetch pur Misyoor Montague a autem bawler—'tis too late fer naught else but the eternity box for 'im anyways."

At Tizzie's reassuring wink, Lizzie reached deep inside her bodice and pulled out a leather drawstring bag heavy with gold. The crowd of raggedy beggars and narrow-eyed cutthroats concentrated their attention on the bag Lizzie held aloft, and it took no more than a second for one of their number to make a grab for it—the man with the open running sores, to be exact.

Instant pandemonium broke loose in the gin shop on the ground floor of number fourteen as the leather pouch came undone and a shower of gold guineas rained down among the crowd, who dropped to their knees to scrabble in the filth after the bouncing, rolling coins.

"Now!" Kit hissed to Ozzy, breaking from the shadows as Del stood in the doorway and waved the all-clear. As Tizzie and Lizzie, their part in the scheme completed, were led out of the shop by Bob, who had been commissioned with the job of returning the ladies safely to Berkeley Square, Kit and Ozzy slid into the gin shop undetected, squeezed past the mass of humanity pummeling each other on the floor, and passed through the door Ben had promised them led to a stairway to the upper floors. When Kit took one last look back into the shop it was to see Montague, his gunshot-rent, bloody shirt easy to spot in the fray, happily knocking heads together as if it were the greatest of good fun. "Come to me, little cabbage," Kit heard the chef croon, stalking the tapster who had refused a dying man sanctuary, and the earl only wished he could stay and watch more of the melee.

The sounds of the fight reached the ears of Tiny and Goliath, who had been standing at the rear of number fourteen waiting for precisely that signal to begin their part of the rescue. "Up we go," Goliath chortled as Tiny boosted his small friend up to the windowsill far above them. Goliath disappeared for a moment, only to reappear at the back door into the alley, which he had opened from the inside. "In ya get, Tiny," he whispered from the darkness. "Hoist me up now, friend— we's ta track up the dancers afore that Ives cove can trig it outta 'ere. We'll teach 'm ta snaggle our missus!"

*   *   *

Ives had been busy composing an inspired note to Lord Bourne detailing instructions on the delivery of the ransom when the commotion from the ground floor reached the apartment on the fourth floor. Sending one of his fellows downstairs to check on the noise, Ives was not best pleased to see his captive smiling at him, obviously certain that her rescue was at hand.

"I warned you, Mr. Ives," Jennie said pleasantly. "You will soon be prodigiously sorry you have gone up against my husband. He's been mentioned in dispatches, you know, for his bravery in battle. I do believe you are about to see all your nasty plans fall to pieces. Perhaps he will go easy on you if you release me now. Else"—she shrugged diffidently—"I vow I will not be held accountable for the consequences. Lord Bourne has a fearsome temper when he's been crossed."

Ives did not like the effect Jennie's calm assurance had on his two remaining hirelings. Damn the woman anyway, he thought fiercely. She's supposed to be crying and swooning, not sitting there grinning like a child who's just been handed a birthday treat. Didn't the chit know anything? So far the only fear she'd shown at all was to worry that everyone else would be worrying about her. It just wasn't natural, Ives reflected, giving the countess a nasty look, and besides, it took all the fun out of the thing. If he was going to have to gather up the ransom and flee the country the least she could do was act as if he intimidated her a little bit.

When his cohort came back to say that it was a big to-do about nothing, only some fistfight among the customers of the gin shop, Ives felt it was his turn for a little gloating. "So much for your awe-

inspiring soldier husband, madam. There'll be no
rescue, only a gentlemanly exchange—his money
for your life. No one knows you're here, you know,
and even if they did it wouldn't do them any
good. I can just see it now—the high and mighty
Earl of Bourne sauntering down Cow Cross Street,
sticking out like a sore thumb. He'd have his
throat slit in a minute for his trouble." The man's
features turned hard as he attempted to wipe the
smile from Jennie's face once and for all. "Now
shut up, or your husband is going to be paying
good money for a lifeless corpse."

But it was Jennie who got in the last word. "I
doubt it, Mr. Ives. Kit wouldn't pay a bent penny
for you—dead or alive!"

The steep, narrow stairs led up into the darkness, twisting and turning as they rose past three
floors of apartments that Ben told his master
were rented out by the month, the day, and, at
times, the hour, for any number of reasons—none
of them very savory. By the time the small party
reached the fourth floor, Ozzy was holding a
scented handkerchief to his nose to smother the
combined smell of cooked cabbage, old sweat, and
human waste. The tilted floor creaked slightly as
they tiptoed across it, heading for the nearest
door. Kit put his ear to it, listening for some
sound, and then stepped a few paces back, clearly
intending to break down the barrier with his
shoulder, but Ben stopped him just before he
could fling his body against the wood. " 'ere now,
guv'nor, iffen ya wants ta dub the jigger, 'ow
'bout usin' the locksmith's daughter?" the former
pickpocket asked quietly, dangling a large set of
keys in front of Kit's eyes invitingly.

"Ben's a right fine dimber damber man, ain't

'e, guv'nor?" Del whispered, obviously proud of Ben's talent in relieving the tapster of his keys. "It's proud Oi am wot knows 'im."

While Ozzy stuffed his handkerchief into his mouth to stifle his mirth, Kit bowed his head to Ben and took possession of the keys. Silent as a band of mice tiptoeing over cotton wadding, Kit turned lock after lock along the long hallway, trial and error showing him that a single brass key fit all the doors. All but two of the rooms were empty, with a snoring drunk and a couple lost in each other and unaware of any intrusion being the sole inhabitants of the other rooms.

But when they reached the second-to-the-last door near the end of the hall, Kit motioned that he could hear voices on the other side of the wooden barrier. Pocketing the set of keys, Kit chose to crash through the door by running against it full tilt with his shoulder, a move that caught the four men inside the room unawares and served to set loose a rousing cheer from the female tied up in the corner. Unfortunately, this move also caused Kit to cannon out of control all the way to the far wall, and while Ozzy quickly nabbed one of Ives's hirelings and Ben and Del succeeded in tackling and sitting on the second, the third man and Ives scrambled out the doorway untouched.

Dropping a quick kiss on the end of his wife's nose, Kit ran back the way he had come in time to see that Ives and the last man had split up, the hireling heading for the back stairs (and the waiting Tiny), and Ives choosing to escape via the front stairs that led to the gin shop. "Watch Jennie!" Kit called back over his shoulder as he made a grab for the rickety stair rail and set off in pursuit of Ives, anger lending wings to his feet.

Ives had reached the ground floor and had taken two steps into the gin shop when Kit, launching himself like a pouncing tiger, caught him from the back, the two of them tumbling into the middle of the fight that was just then winding down. As Kit dragged Ives to his feet and set himself in a sparring attitude, the crowd quickly formed a circle around the two combatants, eager to see what looked to be a fine display of cross-and-jostle work.

They were not to be disappointed. Both Bourne and Ives had studied under Gentleman Jackson, and being much of the same size and weight, the men put on a much better show than any mill in recent memory. But anger lent strength to Kit's punches, and it was not long before Dean Ives lay sprawled against the bar, his legs splayed out in front of him as he lapsed into unconsciousness. While Kit stood at the ready, more than willing to go a few more rounds, Ben entered the room and, looking about happily, spied a nearby slop jar, the contents of which he dumped over Ives's head, supposedly to revive him.

The ring of onlookers, still cheering over the spectacle, parted then, and Goliath came bounding into the room, doing handsprings as he made a path for the giant Tiny, who was carrying the third hireling under his arm like a sack of grain. "I be done wit 'im now," Tiny told the earl, dropping the unconscious man at Kit's feet. "D'ya be wantin' 'im dead, master? 'e's jist sleepin' fer now, but I be 'appy ta fix that iffen ya jist give Tiny the word."

Sight of the huge black man had the customers of the gin shop at number fourteen thinking wistfully of their homes and beds, and the crowd thinned rapidly, leaving the tapster quite alone to face the strangers in his midst. "Makes me no nevermind," that man piped up helpfully to answer Tiny's question. "Jist git 'em outta 'ere, an' Jack Gooden'll keep mum about it."

"I'll just bet you will," Kit opined thinly, his level stare effectively wiping the smile from the tapster's face. "Why don't you be a good fellow and play least in sight for a bit, hmmm?" Kit suggested smoothly, and the man, wiping his broad hands nervously on his leather apron, backed hurriedly toward the open door to the street.

"Take care of things here," Kit ordered Ben, turning toward the stairs once more, looking every inch the earl even dressed as he was in Renfrew's shabby gardening clothes, intent on returning to his kidnapped bride and thus missing Tiny's actions as, following Ben's orders, the giant picked up Ives with one hand and hung the man on a hook by the collar of his stylish jacket.

Kit ran up the stairs two at a time, dabbing a trickle of blood from the cut on his cheek lest Jennie fly into the boughs demanding he see a doctor. Bursting into the room down the hall from the fourth landing, a bit breathless from both the fight with Ives and his long climb, his eyes searched out Jennie, who was rubbing her wrists where her bonds had so recently been. "*Kitten!*" he shouted, breaking into a wide grin as the sound of his voice had her blond head jerking upward, her beautiful face alight with joy.

"*Kit!*" she exclaimed, hopping to her feet and pitchforking herself into his widespread arms. "I *knew* you would come for me."

Raining kisses over her face and neck, Kit at last gave in to the fear that he had felt at thinking he had lost her—lost his darling kitten—and as Jennie's arms closed tightly around his neck he growled fiercely, "Oh, my love. My dearest, dearest love. I'll never let you out of my sight again! I adore you, my little kitten."

Ozzy clamped his hands down over Del's ears and turned the footman toward the door. "Come with me, my good man. You're too young to see this. Besides, it does me a bad turn to see one of my own kind drooling and slobbering like some lovesick calf." So saying, Ozzy Norwood shepherded his charge and their two captives out of sight of the loving couple and in the direction of the gin shop and more manly pursuits—like trussing up the baddies and hauling them off to the roundhouse before going somewhere private and getting themselves roaring drunk.

It wasn't until much later, shed of their well-wishers, bathed, fed, and snuggled up together in the large bed in the master chamber in Berkeley Square, that Jennie brought up a subject that had been teasing at her mind. "Kit, darling," she crooned, lazily marching her fingers up his bare chest, "about Mr. Ives's helpers. They were not a very nice sort, you understand, but there was this one young one . . ."

"Oh?" Kit urged, his intuition telling him he had better gather his wits about him before she spoke again.

"Yes," she went on thoughtfully. "They gagged me, you know, until I promised not to scream. The young one—I think his name was Hughie—he used my own handkerchief when I protested about the dirty rag they were planning to use. He was so young, Kit," she went on, shifting slightly to look up into her husband's eyes imploringly.

"Not a hardened criminal, surely. So I was thinking. . ."

The Earl of Bourne, feeling a comforting warmth growing deep in his chest, merely smiled and sighed, "Go on, kitten. I'm listening."

Epilogue

Sir Cedric Maitland was in his glory, dandyling his grandson Christopher on his knee while his proud parents looked on fondly. "Do you like that, Christopher?" the man asked the toothless, smiling infant. "One day soon I'll take you riding to hounds with me."

"What?" Kit asked, feigning shock. "With your disky heart?"

"What disky heart?" his father-in-law blustered before ducking his head sheepishly. "Oh, that. I was only funning with you, son, didn't you know?"

"I knew," Kit answered softly, lifting his wife's hand to his lips.

Sir Cedric relaxed and decided to take credit for his daughter's happy marriage. "You'd have gotten around to marrying my baby girl sooner or later. I just helped things along a bit."

Jennie laughed at her papa's silliness and went back to the mail sitting in her lap. Spying her cousin Lucy's childish scrawl, she opened the letter and steeled herself to decipher the crossed lines dotted with inky blotches and crossed-out words. "Oh dear," she sighed at last, putting the letter down.

"What's your cousin up to this time?" Kit asked, taking in his wife's frown. "Don't tell me she's still chasing poor old Thorpe all over creation."

"It's ten times worse than that, darling. It seems Lord Thorpe has somehow been turned out of society in disgrace and Lucy, that dear, sweet girl, has sworn to clear his good name."

Kit cocked his head to one side. "That's our Lucy—never say die."

"Well, I think she's wonderfully brave!" Jennie declared, rising to pick up Christopher and kiss him before handing the child over to the loving care of Tizzie and Lizzie. "Time for your nap, sweetness," she crooned, nuzzling the infant's chubby neck, "and time for our luncheon."

As they adjourned to the dining room arm in arm behind Sir Cedric, Kit kissed Jennie's temple and soothed, "Don't fret, kitten. If I know Lucy, and I'm afraid I do, London is about to be set on its collective heels!"

"Yes, love." Jennie smiled back happily. "And Lord Thorpe—I wonder how he'll fare, once Lucy gets the bit between her teeth."

Kit chuckled at the thought. "I can't say for sure, but I'll wager my best hunter the toplofty Lord Thorpe will never know what hit him!"

"Poor man," Jennie giggled, her green eyes dancing. "What I wouldn't give to be there when his lordship realizes Lucy intends to become a dragon in his defense."

"I'm afraid you'll have to miss the fun, pet, as Christopher and I have need of you here. Most especially me. Didn't you say you were going to show me your secret place in the Home Wood this afternoon?" he said, waggling his eyebrows at her conspiratorially. "The place nobody else can find where you like to lie on the soft grass and gaze up at the sky through the overhanging trees?"

"Why, Christopher Wilde," Jennie simpered suggestively, leaning into his shoulder as he pulled out her chair. "Whatever do you have in mind?"

"Dessert, my dear," he whispered in her ear, sending a delicious tingle up her spine. "Just a little dessert."

"What a lovely idea," Jennie breathed softly, blushing like a young maiden as her papa discreetly coughed into his napkin, pretending he hadn't heard a single word of the lovers' exchange.

Supremely satisfied with himself and the world at large, he then leaned back comfortably in his chair, silently hoping that Montague had prepared his favorite strawberry tarts for dessert. To each generation its own idea of pleasure, Sir Cedric heartily believed, and at *his* age, downing three strawberry tarts—his and Jennie's and Kit's—in one sitting was all the adventure he could stand. With any luck at all, he then told himself complacently, making yet another wish as out of the corners of his eyes he watched Kit and his daughter gazing into each other's eyes like moonstruck calves, young Christopher is not destined to be my only grandchild.

Happily, as it turned out, Sir Cedric was not to be disappointed on either count.

About the Author

Michelle Kasey is the pseudonym of Kasey Michaels, which is the pseudonym of Kathie Seidick, a suburban Pennsylvania native who is also a full-time wife and the mother of four children. Her love of romance, humor, and history combine to make Regency novels her natural medium.

Other Regency Romances from SIGNET

                                                             (0451)
☐ THE INCORRIGIBLE RAKE by Sheila Walsh.   (131940—$2.50)
☐ THE DIAMOND WATERFALL by Sheila Walsh.   (128753—$2.25)
☐ THE RUNAWAY BRIDE by Sheila Walsh.   (125142—$2.25)
☐ THE INCOMPARABLE MISS BRADY by Sheila Walsh.   (135687—$2.50)
☐ THE ROSE DOMINO by Sheila Walsh.   (136616—$2.50)
☐ THE AMERICAN BRIDE by Megan Daniel.   (124812—$2.25)
☐ THE UNLIKELY RIVALS by Megan Daniel.   (110765—$2.25)
☐ THE RELUCTANT SUITOR by Megan Daniel.   (096711—$1.95)
☐ AMELIA by Megan Daniel.   (094875—$1.75)

Prices slightly higher in Canada

on next page for ordering.
bookstore or use coupon
on last page for ordering.

More Regency Romances from SIGNET

**Buy them at your local
bookstore or use coupon
on next page for ordering.**